THE NIGHT DOCTOR

CULE HINDER

Other books by the author (also available on kindle)
DARK SIDE CROSSING
THE EIGHTH SQUARE
THE VIXEN
THE LAWYER'S TALE
Coming soon:
JAKARTA MONKEYS
THE MUMMER'S SONG
THE DRAGON'S TALE

Cover art "Zoya" © Gloria Hindle

CHAPTER 1

George squinted up at the Heathrow Departures Board. Don't say his sight was going too. He was already sensitive about the tufts of surgically replaced hair on his shining red crown. Just then his mobile phone rang; the name MARTY showed on the screen. He sighed but put the phone to his ear and answered jovially, "Georgie!"

"How ya doing came the gruff, transatlantic tones of his boss. The bank was a partnership but, as the eldest and most experienced, Marty got the accolade of "boss"

"I'm great! Never better!"

"Careful how you go over there," Marty said, "those guys aren't the patsies they seem."

Since when did he need a lecture on how to handle a target? Maybe he'd misfired a couple of times lately but he had his domestic problems and there was no reason for the main man to be on his case. "Leave it to me," he said, "they'll be eating out of my hand."
They bantered on a bit then said their goodbyes. George put two fingers up. One mistake, that's all he'd made, one mistake, and they were checking up on his every move.

His phone rang again. This time HOME appeared.
What did Jen want now? Yes, he was late with the
maintenance but she'd set the Rottweiler on him.
Pissing the kids' inheritance down the legal sewer was
how he saw it. He pressed the NO button, cackling
mischievously. An air stewardess, tugging her cabin
baggage behind her, looked at him askance. His eyes
followed her. Phew, he thought, she's all right, which
was precisely the sort of thought which had put him in
the estranged category to start with. As for the wife, let
her sweat. The last time they spoke she'd called him a
bully. And he'd never laid a finger on her! He might
have got his leg over a couple of times but that's the
way it was in his job - there was always fanny throwing
itself at him. "It's not my fault if I'm irresistible," he
said aloud and more than one passer-by turned and
looked at the strange man talking to himself. He made
faces and ran his hand gingerly through his hair,
grimacing as he felt the smoothness of the growing bald
patch. He hoped that surgery would work.

It was then that he saw the Tory politician, Ken Clark.
A grin crossed his face; he was just about to move in
and make some cheeky comment about the amount of
tax he paid when he realised the Cabinet Minister was
arguing with a woman whom he presumed to be his
wife. The couple had to change terminals and Ken was
giving it large about how it was her fault. George
wanted to rise to her defence and tell Ken off. The
politician was bent double over a luggage trolley which

was absolutely chocker-block full of gear. "Doing a moonlight are yous?" George shouted, a big grin on his face, his accent reverting to his native Geordie for this jibe. Mr. Clark turned and looked at him, his face perspiring profusely. He bent double as he tried to manoeuvre the trolley. His backside was stuck up in the air like a duck's diving for fish. George was tempted to kick it as the politician moved past. It was a temptation but he just managed to control it. The couple receded into the distance, not bickering quite so hard now they knew they were on show.

He squinted up at the board again. Going blind would be a bigger bummer even than going bald. You can't surgically replace your eyes! He could see there was a check-in number but it was swimming like a dolphin. He made it out eventually and trundled off to the check-in gate. When he got there he began to feel better, perhaps something to do with the blond checking the boarding cards. Whoa! It was the air-hostess who had crossed his path when the wife rang. Jesus, if they all look like her in Lithuania, he would be well in! His turn came in the queue. "All right, sweetheart?" he said as she took his card.

"Business Class. Please board at the front, sir," the stewardess smiled in reply.

"Call me Georgie, petal," he breezed. "Is that where yous'll be?" Again the Geordie accent was coming out. He hailed from the North East but usually liked to act the sophisticated Cockney. "I'm gannin where yous're gannin." She laughed at him and joshed him along. "I'll be looking out for yous," he called back to her, "hey, yous're beautiful yous!"

He breezed his way on to the plane, grinning at the other passengers, some of whom coughed politely. Business Class was full of big, dark men. Two of them looked at him closely, their eyes heavily hooded. He wouldn't want to meet either of them down a dark alley. "Heaven, I'm in heaven," he began to sing when he discovered the blond was indeed the Business Class stewardess. He grabbed her sleeve as she passed. "Who are all these heavy guys?" he asked.

She looked a little alarmed but decided to humour him. "There's a diplomatic convention in Vilnius. All the former Warsaw Pact countries are represented."

"Warsaw Pact? I thought that went out with the ark!"

"Not exactly, Lithuania's only been an independent republic since 1991! A little post-ark don't you think?"

The wit wasn't entirely lost on him. "Jesus, only that long! What was it before?"

She did a double take. The English had the reputation of being insular but surely he couldn't be that thick? "It was part of the U.S.S.R!"

"Just testing yous, hen. I knew that really."

"Ah, you're quite a joker, sir! I can see that! And what are you travelling to Lithuania for?"

"I'm an investment banker!" He figured that would impress her and he said it loud enough, also, for others to hear. A nice air hostess to show you the sights (internal and external if you were lucky) was always a bit of a male traveller's fantasy.

"And you have business in Vilnius?" She was suddenly interested.

"Sure do, sweetheart, very good news for your country. I'm going there to set up a multi-million dollar deal. My Bank is investing fortunes. Plenty of jobs, plenty of wealth." He rubbed the index finger and thumb of his right hand together and she looked at it a little perplexed, as if it were a vaguely pornographic gesture.

"Good," she replied, "but you must excuse me, I have to look after these other gentlemen."

"Yeah, but you've got to be especially nice to me. Because all those people we're investing in are depending on you!"

"I'll try and make a special case of you, Georgi!" She added the hard G of the Russian pronunciation. He quite liked that. Meanwhile, one of the diplomats had been looking his way while he sweet-talked the stewardess. He'd clocked the attention and that's why he'd talked the situation up: a sort of eat-your-heart-out-Ivan ploy; I'm the man, rich, successful and pulling the lasses. The stranger leaned across and handed him a card, which revealed him to be a member of the Russian Embassy. "Top of the morning to you too!" George responded and shook the man's hand. He was thinking about the guy's resemblance to Yeltsin. Did they all look like that?

"I heard what you were saying there," the diplomat said in a thick Russian accent. "Maybe we can do each other some good?"

"What d'you have in mind?" George went into negotiating mode. He just loved to deal!

"You are investment banker? And you invest in Lithuania?"

"Maybe. It looks like it, unless a wheel comes off?"

"A wheel?" The Russian didn't seem to get the metaphor.

"Figure of speech.. I mean provided nothing goes wrong in the d.d."

"The DD?" The Russian looked perplexed.

George sighed like one surrounded by imbeciles. "I'm talking about the due diligence."

"Ah!" The man nodded. He had those heavy Russian eyelids, real gangster droopies. "First time?"

"First time? Oh you mean first investment in Lithuania? Oh yeah, first time."

"You ever invest in Russia? Plenty opportunity."

"I've heard it's dicey, too much black economy? They call it the wild, wild east, huh?"

"Depend who you know!" The diplomat looked annoyed at George's dismissal of his country as a lawless backwater.

"You mean someone like you?"

"Call me," the Russian said.

"Maybe." George tried to introduce a note of coolness into it. "If I've got the time. If I don't do this deal." He looked at the card but only perfunctorily.

The Russian didn't appear to much like the suggestion that he was no more than a backstop opportunity. "Maybe you will, maybe you won't," he muttered. "If you ever finish this deal." He said the last sentence with a touch of venom as if it were a warning.

George was puzzled as the man turned away. "Why shouldn't I?" he asked. The man didn't reply. "Hey fella, come on! Put up or shut up! Why shouldn't I finish this deal?"

The Russian turned round and looked him piercingly in the eye. "I feel this deal in Lithuania is a bad deal."

"Why?" George's mouth dropped open like a fly-trap, as it tended to when he was surprised.

The Russian turned to his neighbour and addressed George with his back to him. "Maybe it's just you look like a man whose luck has run out."

"What do you mean?" George blustered, shocked not only by the change but also by the intimacy of the Russian's statement. The latter and his even fatter companion grinned. The fat man made with his fore and middle fingers as if to put a gun to his head and then with his thumb as if to pull the trigger.

The tension the encounter might have created was relieved because the stewardess, oblivious to all that had gone on, came and sat next to him for take-off. There was a spare seat there, but he kidded himself she had a choice and he was it. He turned and winked at the Russians. His look said, eat your heart out cocksuckers! These girls recognise class when they see it. "Tell me something about your country?" he said to her brightly.

She obliged with a brief rundown of the geography, the demographics and the economic climate and, just as he was about to fall asleep, she mentioned an old folk's tale from her home region. Half-listening, in a kind of catatonic state, the rush of the world having caught up with him, her voice lulled him into unconsciousness like a mother her child. He picked up a bit about a castle, a prince and princess and an evil king who killed the prince and stole the princess but lost his soul on the way. It seemed a very complicated story and a bit too fantastic for his taste and he found himself drifting away.

The stewardess had long gone when, vaguely, as if in a dream, he heard the pilot announce that the plane was about to hit some turbulence and recommended the passengers keep seat belts fastened. George hadn't unfastened his. He never did unless he was networking round the plane spreading bonhomie. He prided himself on being a great flyer and he was soon back in a troubled sleep.

A creature came and pointed at him. In the dream it was an angel. It was standing in front of an ancient tree whose arms spread in strange deformities like the curling black smoke of an invisible fire. Next to it was another tree. He understood in the dream that the first tree was an oak and the second a lime and they had a connection but he didn't understand what it was. He wasn't even sure where that information came from but the logic of the dream said it was part of the story the girl had told, which he also remembered in the dream as if his subconscious mind had taken it in.

This angel wasn't friendly; it carried a hammer in one hand; it was strangely androgynous with male and female characteristics. George stood naked and trembling. He was conscious of wanting to wake up but for some reason he couldn't. The angel called him Georgi in rasping tones which reverberated in his head. Its eyes were like an owls' eyes, a semaphore lamp blinking on and off. Fear made him run from oak to lime, hoping to find a hiding place. Beneath each tree he found his place already taken: at the first by a black cow; at the second by a black goat; also at each tree were dark people, clothed in heavy, peasant robes. They held out jugs of ale and he wasn't sure if he should quaff but felt that, if he did, it would be all up with him. A fire burned; something was cooking. He could smell roasting meat. But the beast being cooked looked distinctly like a man….He awoke to find the plane rattling. It lurched suddenly; a prolonged scream came from the rear. It lifted and jumped, smitten by some godlike hand. He quickly lost touch with the bumps as fear drained every sense. He'd been on some air journeys in his time but nothing like this. The stewardess came out of the serving compartment as green as angelica and stumbled down the aisle. He didn't even think of getting up to help. Male or female, the chivalry bit went out of the window at this point. The plane banked; the stewardess strapped herself in next to him. George felt strangely angry about that. Wasn't she supposed to be helping them - correction, him? It could be a life or death situation. She wasn't allowed to be human, she was a professional! "Oh, Jesus," he said, "please help me."

It occurred to him that Jen would be gloating. It was daft the things that went through your head at times like this. His share options would make her rich! He hadn't changed his bloody will! "I'll bet she's wished this on me," he thought aloud, and then he remembered Jen didn't actually have an evil bone in her body. If she was coming across as tough, it was him who'd made her stand up for herself. Then the pilot announced they were diverting round the storm, which would add a little time to the journey. He sounded ridiculously calm. "Don't tell us pal, just do it," George shouted back at the invisible intercom.

CHAPTER 2

The shadows could have swallowed Scandinavia. Cool
and green near the moonlight which filtered through the
arched windows, they stretched away as black as
octopus ink towards the forest, which was always there,
always on the edge of everything in this country. It was
like a gateway into a different world, one inhabited by
strange beings from the brothers Grimm, or by knights
in white surplices adorned with the black cross *patté*.

Dry coughing disturbed the interminable silence of the
corridors and this staccato interruption was followed by
a metallic, un-oiled squeak. The invisible, offending
object approached the top of the corridor where a sign
read "*Morgas*" in the Lithuanian language. Nowadays it
meant the place where dead bodies are kept before
interment, rather than a place where they are retained
until identified, although the hospital morgue had
fulfilled both functions in its time. The source of the
sound became clear as an empty trolley appeared,
pushed by a shuffling male figure. Tall and dark, he
walked with the slow, exaggerated movements of long
limbs until he drew abreast of a room and stopped. The
night porter's vigil was a lonely one and the ghostly
shadows in the radiating spurs of the hospital wings
were getting to him. What had the night doctor said the
shadows reminded her of? The sleeping bodies of those

dear, departed friends. The ones we could not save. The light went on in the next room and another went on in his heart. It was the night doctor and she was putting on her white coat.

She smiled at the porter, whom she'd known since the Communists ran the hospital. This was not that long ago but it was also like time immemorial in the new, free Baltic psyche. "Vytautus," she said without exclamation, as if she had expected him to be there, "I may have a little job for you soon. A slightly unusual assignment." The only giveaway was her lowered voice. Vytautus pricked up his ears. It must be a sensitive matter because the night doctor always addressed him in these hushed tones when she wanted no stranger to hear. He'd do anything for her. Then she added, "Something in the body disposal department?" She said it matter-of-factly as if it were a question and so it was. Epidemics come and go: geriatrics out of winter fuel; drunks dying of exposure; children with tuberculosis - the restless ebb and flow of life. No point being sentimental about it. He indicated to let her know he would be there when she needed him and she walked, more like a mannequin than a hospital doctor, towards the wards. She remembered something and turned back. "How is Natalie?" she asked.

He opened his hands in a gesture of thanksgiving. "Wonderful!" he exclaimed.

"She must be a big girl now. What, fifteen?" He nodded

and she smiled. It was good to have successes. They made the heavy burden of the failures much easier to bear.

She walked down to the children's ward, not liking the sound of coughing from one of the cots. Poor mite, she was thinking. The child's choking eased almost as soon as the night doctor touched him. She could make people feel better just by showing them she was there. She had this gift with all people, old people, young people, it didn't matter, but she didn't fool herself. It could have been worse: at least the Russians had gone; and the country had not passed through the same nightmares as some of the other fledgling republics. That's what we are, she thought, workers in the industry of bereavement, the biggest employer in the world.

She finished her shift when the angelus called her to the hospital chapel for the first devotion of the day in honour of the Incarnation of Christ. She lit a candle and prayed for all those for whom her help had proved all too human. She hung up her coat and was about to leave the hospital, dog-tired after another long shift, when Vytautus told her that General Antonov had called on the off chance of catching her before she left. She couldn't hide her surprise nor the degree of pleasure. The General had been the Commander-in-Chief of the Soviet forces in the Baltic. The Cold War years had seen many atrocities but Antonov had earned the gratitude of the population when he had refused Gorbachev's command to turn his tanks on the

Landsbergis Parliament. The night doctor had known him from before that Spring of 1991. Their first encounter came when she saved his son's life at the age of fifteen. The boy had been injured in a motor accident. The operation had been touch and go but he'd pulled through. The general now revered her as some kind of saint.

"Mikhail," the doctor said, a radiant smile on her face. Gallantly he brushed her hand with his lips. "What brings you here? How is Dimitri?"

His hands slipped to his side in a gesture of despair, and he replied, "Alas, you saved him only for the army to make cannon fodder of him!"

"Oh no," she cried, her hand pressed to her mouth in horror. "How?"

"Chechnya!"

She was struck with the fact that people cannot escape their destiny. We can run from it, we can hide for a time, but we can never cheat it. Those who succeed for the longest time are often hunted people, merely a pale imitation of themselves, frightened of their own shadows.

Once she had recovered it became clear that the general had a dual purpose in coming to see her. "I know this may come as a surprise. You have not seen me for some time. But I wonder....." His voice trailed off with apparent anxiety.

She was amused to think that this paradigm of machismo, a man who had for a time controlled his own private army, was now lost for words. She kept her amusement to herself. "Yes?"

"I wonder if you would consider coming out with me one evening?" He looked at her, hoping.

"I would be delighted."

The answer came as a surprise. He had prepared for rejection and now looked almost boyish. "Tonight, for dinner? We could go to the theatre perhaps? Do you still have that interest?"

"Oh yes," she laughed, "some things never change."

"I have been thinking, now that I am retired, it is an interest I would like to follow up more."

"Surely you are too young to retire!"

"You are too kind," the general responded, "but I am retired from active service. I retain a consultancy role. I am here for a week, observing the conference."

"Oh, the Warsaw Pact nonsense?" she replied.

"The last rites of the Warsaw Pact. It's all up this week. NATO has won." She contemplated this titbit of information with nothing like the same nostalgia as he felt. The West might not be perfect but between its open society and what they had endured there was simply no contest. An unstoppable right had overcome an immovable might. "Tonight, for dinner?" he added, "and then the theatre if there is anything on? I would love that."

She shook her head. "I cannot tonight. I have another engagement." Vytautus was shuffling past behind her and their eyes hooked each other's. A secret exchange, of which the general was oblivious, passed between them.

"Tomorrow then?" He was unsure if this was a different kind of brush off.

"Tomorrow would be lovely. I start my time off now." She scribbled down a number for him to call her and he went away on a cushion of air, warbling the song of the Volga Boatmen. She raised her eyebrows at his retreating figure. He had a fine voice but she hoped he wasn't thinking of her.

CHAPTER 3

The aeroplane limped into the airport. After disembarking George scanned the waiting faces. He'd spoken to Tomas once from London but had never met him. One of his oppos who had done the face-to-face said the lad wasn't a bit like he'd imagined, which was big and blond with Viking horns coming out of his helmet. If anything he was a bit of a wuss.

"What do you mean by that?" George had asked. "Backs to the wall, like?"

"Well, no, not exactly, just he's a bit effeminate. They are Scandinavians, aren't they? Not what you'd expect of a Scandi."

"Maybe there was a boat in the fjord, that night?" George had quipped.

"Do they have fjords in Lithuania?"

I give up, George thought, and the joke was lost. Anyway the report was excellent, which is why he'd chosen Tomas as the dupe.

No one came out of the crowd, which added to his ill-humour. From the fact-file, Tomas was in his twenties;

he remembered the photograph on his company website: on this his contact's face had an unnaturally pale hue, as if he were consumptive, but photos could be deceptive. He looked anxiously around. A scruffy man in a fawn coloured leather jacket approached. "You American?" he asked. George looked back at him with barely concealed disgust.

"Brit," he replied curtly.

The man's face creased in a grin, a passable impression of a wolf. "Little American! You want ride into city? I take." He grabbed George's arm.

"Get off!" George pulled away, but the man was persistent and held him near the funny bone, between finger and thumb. It caused a peculiar feeling, like acupuncture, which George had contracted once in Hong Kong.

"I take!" He made a grab for George's bag. George clutched the briefcase. He wasn't parting company with that. It contained dynamite information about the deal. In the wrong hands things could get very nasty. The opposition would know his whole game plan. The man seemed to sense he had something valuable in there but grabbed his suitcase instead.

"It doesn't matter," George said, near to panic, "I'm meeting someone." The man leered at him, then, with relief, George heard a shout. An earnest, bespectacled face peered over the heads in front, and it looked vaguely like the screen-shot he'd seen of Tomas. If so he was searching for his VIP passenger. He held up his arm and waved. Tomas responded and started to push through the melee. The unsavoury man gave him a filthy look and slunk into the crowd. George blew out in undisguised relief. "How you doing kid? Pleased to meet ya!" he enthused as Tomas pumped his hand.

"So nice to have you here!" The lad seemed to have good English, which is what his oppo had said. Just as well he could communicate because the local language was diabolical. Not that George was any linguist but he could usually pick up a word or two, enough to get round, but this one was impenetrable. He'd read somewhere in his brief that it was close to the ancient Indo-European languages like Sanskrit and Latin. He liked to get some gen on any place he was visiting and that had lifted itself off the page. That and the fact the place had once been run by something called the Livonian Brotherhood of the Sword. George was fascinated by anything martial because he had always been a bit on the small side as a kid and now he had a sedentary job he liked to pump iron and think he was hard. "You arrived just in time," he said, "I had a so called taxi driver there who just wouldn't take no for an answer."

Tomas ignored him in the sort of way which suggested his way with the language was to lead; he was less comfortable when following. "I hope the flight delay has not altered your faith in our country. It is really auspicious that this is your first visit to Lithuania."

"First of many if we do this deal but I could have done without that flight!"

Again Tomas pointedly ignored the personal part of the message. "Oh, we will do this deal," he replied, "let me take your bag."

George let him take his suitcase but still clung to the briefcase. Tomas had intended carrying both bags for his honoured guest but backed off. George noticed that his oppo had been right but, despite Tomas's distinctly soft appearance, he was as strong as the taxi driver. He was embarrassed with his own rebuff. "Hey, all the secrets of the operation, can't let this out of my sight!" He regretted that; he shouldn't have given away that he had secrets. Why was he talking so much? Shut it! He told himself fiercely.

But Tomas didn't seem to have noticed. "Sure," he replied, "so we get you to your hotel. It is nearly 9.30. It is going to take time to get out of the airport. There is a conference in the city. The official cars leave first. We have an early start tomorrow, a meeting with the consortium, and I was hoping to run you out to see the new factory in Panevezys."

"Good. But no beating about the bush, have you got the cash, that's what I want to know?"

Tomas smiled a thin smile. It took some time to deliver as if his face muscles were stiff. "The cash?"

"Yeah, the deposit. My bank won't bite if you can't lodge your corner. No changing the goalposts now, kid."

"No, of course not," Tomas said, "I thought you meant I should have some money on me. For you."

"What? A bribe you mean?"

"No, no, not a bribe exactly, a sort of commission. You know, Georgi, it is not long that Lithuania has been a market economy."

"What did you call me?"

"Georgi. Is that okay?"

It was that hard 'G' again. "Yeah, sure. Just reminded me of the air stewardess, that's all."

"The air stewardess?"

"Yeah. She called me that. I think she took a bit of a shine to me." He remembered, though, she'd managed to elude him after the touchdown and he saw that as a missed opportunity. He came back to the present. "What were you saying?"

"The way things were done in the old Soviet Union is not supposed to be the way now. Slowly we are getting rid but...well, old habits die hard. We get some who still make the old demands of us."

"I understand where you're coming from kid, but that's not the way we do business. I've seen those contracts with gratuities for this and commissions for that. I've done deals in the Middle East, the Far East, anywhere you care to mention, but this deal is straight down the middle." He pushed his pointed hand out in front of him to emphasise the fact.

"I am glad to hear it," Tomas replied, as they approached the car. "My board is nervous about having to pay over the deposit before we get the loan. It looks a little…. How do you say …. Not the wrong way round but … He was striving for the words. "Anyway, I mean we would have been happier if both had happened together."

"Well, I understand that, kid, but we have to see the money go into an account before we lodge. We have to be certain you can keep your side up and the cash is clean and locked in. You don't lodge it and then pull it back as soon as we transfer the loan. The problem any country making the transition yours is making has is credibility. We've got to know there's no nasties going to crawl out of the woodwork."

"Yes," Tomas protested genially, "but George there is a month between the transactions. What's the justification?"

"You're changing the goalposts, kid"!" George wagged a finger.

"We have to tie up our money for a month before you put anything down! That seems unfair to me."

"It's not unfair. We have the dollars and you don't. That's the way the world works. Cash is king. There's got to be a delay while we do the due diligence. Before we go to that expense we need to know you're committed. Otherwise the deal could bomb out, leaving us with all the lawyers and accountants to pay. Those guys charge like wounded bulls!"

Tomas shrugged. "Okay!" he said.

"Them's the rules!"

George got a shock when he saw the car they'd sent for him. It was a battered old Trabant, white with red sign-writing on the sides, a flasher unit on top. He looked at Tomas askance. "Is this a cop car?" He pointed at the red writing and yellow beacon.

"No," Tomas laughed, "it's one of the cars the company uses for a Government contract. The writing stands for Waste Disposal Team."

George's lip curled. "You send the frigging waste disposal team to collect me?" His jaw hung slack.

Tomas laughed nervously. "Sorry, George, my car broke down. I had to get someone out after hours because of the flight delay. Best I could do. All the limos in Vilnius are booked for the diplomatic convention." He shrugged and made a gesture of resignation. It didn't create a good impression but there it was - take it or leave it, in which case they could walk into the city but it was a long way. George was irked but couldn't argue with the logic. Then he got his next surprise when the driver of the car got out to put his bag in the boot. It was the wolfish looking man from the arrivals hall. George gaped at him. The other man leered back. "This is our driver, Vytautus," Tomas said.

"I didn't appreciate....I didn't know....." George started to explain. The man ignored him and threw the suitcase in the back of the vehicle in a way that made George think of his wife's collection of Meissen porcelain. "No thanks," he added, and the guy still couldn't prise the briefcase from his grip. Should have handcuffed it on, he was thinking then they wouldn't try but when he looked at this Vytautus person he shuddered. He wasn't big and he was getting on but he was made of wire. This guy would just saw off his hand!

"Something wrong?" Tomas asked, smiling in a puzzled sort of way. He didn't look used to the emotion, his face staying impassive, the muscles not even twitching.

George shook his head, thinking he was a little odd, civilised enough but an oddball. "No, no, just I misunderstood something, kid. It's nothing, honest." They had to wait twenty minutes or so while the official cavalcade got under way. Vytautus sat with his window open, chain-smoking. Finally the police signalled the waiting traffic to move. When they arrived at the hotel, once again George wouldn't let the porter take his briefcase when he came with a trolley. "This baby stays with me," he said tersely and the man nodded and took the other bag.

Tomas asked, "Would you like me to take you out for dinner?" He was tempted. It would be helpful having someone to entertain him and show him around a bit on his first night but Tomas wouldn't be great company. Despite his fresh-faced good looks he looked tired and drawn as if he'd had a hard day. "Your missus keeping you up nights, is she?" he joked, but Tomas didn't appear to get the allusion.

"The lad from the company who did the initial due diligence told me you'd just got married?"

"Oh yes." Tomas nodded enthusiastically even if his face didn't much show it. George was reminded of a bruiser he'd known back in the old days who was known as Polythene Nose.

"Hey look, kid, you get on your way back to your lovely, newlywed wife, I'll be okay tonight, I ate on the plane anyway. Uugh!"

Tomas's reaction was astonishing. He looked frantic. "You mean the food on our Lithuanian planes is not good?" He sounded as if he intended to have a word with the airlines chief.

"Lighten up! You can't be perfect. Just makes you the same as the rest of the world, kid! Here, you take care of things at home. Don't worry about me. We'll meet tomorrow and go over everything. There'll be plenty of time for socialising later."

Tomas beamed happily. "You're sure?" he asked politely.

Not for the first time in this situation, George thought, what if I say, no you pillock, you can bloody well spend your wedding night with me! The poor dope would too. He was tempted but even he couldn't be so cruel. "Sure," he said, and he turned and indicated the streets around him, "is this the town centre?" he asked.

"Yes," Tomas replied, "just down to the left and round the corner. That's where all the action is."

"Action eh?" He nodded his head as if reflecting on that. "Is it safe to go walkabout? I've heard you wouldn't dare in Russia."

Even though he was sitting Tomas stretched his frame
and drew himself up to his full height. "Not a bit like
Russia," he said, "safe as houses!" He seemed pleased
with his use of idiom.

"Fine," George replied, "I might take the night air."

"I will send Vytautus back to run you round." He
indicated the driver who sat smoking in the front of the
cab, the window open, his arm resting on the sill. As his
name was mentioned he looked around and again gave
George his wolfish leer. George shuddered and thought,
no thanks. The truth was he didn't want the wizened old
guy or anyone else for a chaperone because, if he went
out, he'd be looking for the sort of action which might
just offend his host's conservative Baltic sensibilities.
He figured Tomas wouldn't have offered the old guy
unless he wanted to spy on him. That's how it was in
places like this. "No need," he replied, "I'll be okay."

"Well he's on duty anyway," Tomas said, "you won't
notice him, but he'll keep an eye on you."

I might have guessed, George thought, and he
wondered uneasily why that should be necessary if the
place was as safe as houses but he replied graciously
enough, "that makes me feel a whole lot better." Tomas
did not catch the hint of sarcasm but the driver looked
at George and it was like a connection moment, he

could just see the old bat understood. It was not so much the language as the tone.

"And I will call on you eight o'clock tomorrow morning?" Tomas asked.

"Sounds good kid. Don't let that lady of yours get too much sleep!" He laughed at the bemused expression on the young man's face as he tried to work out why his wife shouldn't sleep well. George waited, a big grin on his face, but the penny never dropped. Finally he winked at Tomas, in response to which the younger man tried to wink back but, once again, the machinery was a bit rusty, and he still looked as if he didn't get it. George laughed and sauntered into the hotel lobby.

CHAPTER 4

The hotel room was fine, as good as most places he'd stayed. He had a quick shower and then, just as he'd known he would and why he didn't want Tomas tagging along and cramping his style, he fancied stretching his legs and taking a look at the town. It shouldn't take him long. Vilnius was smaller than most British provincial cities. It was getting late and he wasn't sure how long the bars stayed open; he put his spare cash and the papers from his briefcase inside the room safe and took the lift down to the lobby. Outside he took the direction Tomas had suggested. He heard a vehicle cough into life behind him but thought nothing to it and turned a corner into another dark, long street, which descended the hill round a bend. There was no sign of lights up ahead.

Puzzled, because Tomas had assured him the town centre was nearby, he walked down the pitch black street, rounded the bend and walked until he came to a crossroads. He chose left because the road was still descending that way and walked until he came to the river. He got the shock of his life when a soldier appeared out of the shadows and pointed a rifle at him. "Whoa!" he said, holding his hands up. The soldier barked something at him and he replied, "Sorry, I don't understand." He still had his hands high.

"Papers!" the soldier said tersely.

Thank goodness he'd brought his passport with him! He handed it to the soldier who looked at the photo, then shone a pencil torch on him and, with a satisfied grunt but no other word, handed the passport back and waved him on with a peremptory gesture, as if he was some kind of detritus to be consigned to the waste bin. He felt momentarily angry that this man thought his military uniform gave him some kind of superiority over someone whose boots he wasn't fit even to lick, but the sight of the semi-automatic weapon slung under his arm made him bite his tongue and confine his response to a polite enquiry. "Er...excuse me, you don't know where the bars are....?" The soldier had resumed his sentry post at one end of the bridge and it was obvious he was nervous for some reason because he wheeled and pointed the semi-automatic rifle. George held up his hands again in a gesture of appeasement and licked his lips nervously. "No, I guess not."

He walked on towards what looked like a Government building opposite. It was all lit up and it seemed to take an age to walk past it. He trod quickly, seeing the hosts of young soldiers prowling about. The heavy military presence was sobering. It more than hinted at the seriousness of the agenda, which was the end of the old Warsaw Pact and the realignment of certain of its former members with the NATO powers. That this was happening much to the chagrin of the Russian

Federation explained the tension in the city. The Russians couldn't quite get used to their drop in status, which had been rubbed home to clear, shining transparency by the defection of its press-ganged allies to the opposition team!

George remembered that once he'd arrived in an African state in the middle of a coup d'etat and the soldiers had been like that: young, lithe guys, shouldering arms which could blow a hole in you the size of a barn door and looking like that was exactly what was on their bucket list. That's what it reminded him of. He had the sudden, uneasy impression that the Communists were back. It looked ominous, not good for business.

At last, turning a corner, he came to a street which, despite the lateness of the hour, was thronged with people. Thank God, he thought, breathing a sigh of relief and he started making his way towards them, conscious that he looked the rich westerner, Armani suit, Gucci cufflinks, Prada shoes, the works. Most of the people wore drab clothes as if they didn't have two coins to rub together. They were hanging around outside a bar, on the wall of which hung a bright purple neon sign announcing its name as the *Indigo*. He was just glad he'd found it; Tomas couldn't have posted him in a more out of the way hotel, and yet he'd kidded him on it was right next to the action. He'd have a word with young Tomas tomorrow. It might have been difficult to arrange accommodation with all this diplomatic activity in the city but, best to let the lad know he hadn't come up to the bar, just in case he got ahead of himself, and just to make the sting easier to deliver when he had to do it. Always best to make out it's the fault of the stung, not the stinger.

When he'd made his way over to the entrance beneath the night club's neon sign he had to stand in a line to be frisked. One of the doormen asked him if he carried a gun. "You must be joking, kid," he said and held up his arms for the body search. "What you got here? The Crown Jewels?" He paid the cover charge, in return for which his hand was crudely stamped, an action which made him do a double-take and think these guys were so far back they'd be doing the cave painting next. He made his way upstairs. It was dark inside and it took a few moments to get used to the subdued lighting. The joint was busy enough, heaving with a young crowd, their standard dress blue denim. They were not as trendy or as affluent as you'd find down Stringfellows but every bit as lively. He fought his way to the bar and he thought about something neat and chic, something that would mark him out to any talent that might be lying in wait here as a man of distinction, but he had a thirst on him so he ordered a large one of the local lager. The barman, who sported long, tied back hair, gave him a lingering look over. "What's the matter, kid? You don't see many suits in here?" George had his pugnacious chin on, his lower lip hanging down, his 'don't mess with me' look. He'd been in tougher places than this joint and held his end up. He'd bide his time, see what happened.

"No problem," the barman said.

"You don't need to say it, kid. I know it's no problemo. There's something here for me."

The barman smiled in a self-effacing manner as if he almost regretted drawing attention to himself, or at least that was the way it appeared to George. He began to pull the pint, whilst George looked about him, alert now. He could spot an opportunity a mile off and sensed exactly what he'd articulated: that there was something here for him. He didn't articulate the fact that what he had in mind was something in the loose, promiscuous, female category.

Clocking a group, which had formed itself around a long-haired lady, he had to do a double take to confirm she really was looking at him, even if he couldn't see her eyes through her dark sunglasses. Cool, he thought. He guessed she was no spring chicken but she wasn't more than thirty either. That was a good age. He liked a mature woman, no stranger to sex but maybe not finding it as easy to come by as she used to. Married maybe, the excitement gone from the relationship. She didn't want ties; she wanted fun but most of all she wanted sex. And the more he looked at this one, the more he thought she oozed sex appeal. She seemed to regard him saucily from behind her camouflage and then turn away when he caught her eye, her shades gave her an air of mystery but she was tall, long-haired, and dark, unlike a lot of these Baltic chicks. There was something about her which made him feel a trifle uneasy. He tried to analyse it and it wasn't that she looked dangerous. Lots of chicks like to give themselves that air of mystery so it wasn't that. Maybe it was that he'd never seen her type before but for all that he recognised it. He decided it was simply that she was a hooker and therefore he'd have to be careful as sooner or later there would be a negotiation.

He quaffed a quarter of his pint and held up his glass to her as if offering her a drink. She lowered her head slightly and her eyebrows shot up behind the shades, almost birdlike but not a weak bird, more a bird of prey. They were heavily mascara'ed and her eyes were black as coals. He licked his lips. He just knew she'd be a good time. He kept his eye on her. What would she do? He was debating whether he should make the move but she was with a pretty rough looking crowd, including a couple of lads who looked handy enough to hold their own in Newcastle's West End, where his own roots lay. My, that was a few years back. He felt like a fully qualified Cockney now, or maybe a fully-fledged citizen of the world! The group swelled and moved towards him but she was at the back. There was a momentary commotion around him and it got out of hand, so much so he was caught in the crowd surge and had to push a press of bodies away and shout out, "whoa! Steady on!" He held on to his glass like it was a precious object and downed another draught. It was a canny enough pint, a bit strange tasting though. Then, as the surge returned from the other direction like a wave in a tank which has hit a wall, he took a moment before it hit him to stretch out and put the glass down on the bar counter for safety.

The next moment he found himself buffeted, lifted up bodily in the crowd and moved a few feet away from the bar. Parting a man from his beer, back where he came from, was a dangerous occupation; you took your life in your hands if you went down that path. He knew better, though, than to complain and, when the disturbance ended as quickly as it had begun, the bouncers came through the door and got in the melee, and the crowd disappeared over to the other side of the room, he dusted himself down and made his way back to his pint.

The pony-tailed barman stood pouring drinks and regarded George out of deep, brown, sorrowful eyes, not the slightest bit perturbed by the disturbance but more like someone who just didn't enjoy his job. The memory of that haunted look stayed with him and made him glad he wasn't stuck in a dead end job serving the charva public for a living. As soon as he'd composed himself again and taken a few more quaffs of the cool, golden liquid, he looked around for the woman. He'd rather hoped he'd bump up against her in that crowd and she could ask him then what he was packing but it wasn't to be. He laughed ironically. The tricks the mind played! She was there still but engrossed with others and he figured he'd lost her anyway so he downed his pint, ordering another, but keeping one eye on her just in case. He noticed that she seemed to know everyone in the place. Except me, he thought ruefully.

By the time he'd got his third pint he was feeling woozy, truth be told, but it was then, as if on a magnet, that the woman detached herself from the skin-headed, ear-ringed, denim clad tearaways and crossed the room towards him. Perhaps she'd waited until he had downed a few, which would make him an easier mark, but she'd have to get up early to catch out Georgie!

She moved in an easy, rhythmical way, as if she was used to the catwalk. Mentally he began to rub his hands. "George, you're in here, lad," he said to himself, watching her slinky figure, long dark hair, big passionate lips with ruby lipstick. She still had the shades on. He wasn't bothered about them as long as he could get off a few other items of kit. In fact she could keep them on if she took the rest off; he wasn't bothered about looking in her eyes all lovey-dovey while he gave her six nowt. Then "hi," she said almost languidly as she stood in front of him.

He wasn't sure if that was an indication she spoke a lot of English or just another hook. He hoped she spoke English, it could be a long night otherwise, unless she just wanted to get on with the other in which case language wouldn't come into it. But he still liked a bit of verbal foreplay, even if it was the usual, flattering, simple stuff you got with foreign chicks who couldn't speak much of the language - all laughing and simpering sex talk, telling you how great you are, what a big boy you are. "Hey, how ya doing, kid?" he responded, "my name's George, my friends call me Georgie."

"Georgi," she answered.

His jaw dropped down into slack mode, because she said it just as the air stewardess had. Yes he meant the one who'd managed somehow to avoid him at the airport, although it would be difficult to think of two women from the same ethnic background who looked so different, this one so obviously Slavonic, the other equally clearly Teutonic. He couldn't figure out why the stewardess had done a runner like that. Maybe she was married or something. But why should that make any difference? He had dollars, dollars to buy her plenty of things. But that was the past. "Yeah!" He laughed. "Someone else said that. Yeah, Georgi, call me Georgi."

"Okay Georgi," she replied, still studying him coolly. She held a cigarette in her hand and she stood with her head back as if regarding him quizzically and her left knee overlapped the right like a dancer's, or some kind of performer's. Maybe she did the pole dancing, he thought. It was that kind of pose and it made him lick his suddenly dry lips in anticipation of the night's potential. Just his luck to nail a dancer, a real hard body. His own rose in anticipation. He also liked women smoking. It made them sexier somehow, looser, more carefree, and more immoral. She added, "I'm Zoya."

"I'm English by the way," George said.

"You cannot be serious!" The sarcasm made him grin. She dropped her head slightly down because she was tall, although the stilettos might have had something to do with it, and in this posture he could see over her shades and her eyes arched up at him, suddenly unshuttered, almost like an owl's eyes the way they blinked and opened wide, unafraid to ask questions. She held her head up again and the shutters came down. "So what are you doing here, Georgi?" She said the name as if teasing him, and the ghost of a smile played on her lips as she spoke. She was good with English, in fact she was great.

"Looking for action, kid," George replied, and he clicked his tongue and his fingers in unison.

"You've found it." She looked at her empty glass.

"Oh yeah, what you having Zoya?" She wanted a vodka and something which the barman seemed to recognise. "Hey, you're not one of them girls I get charged for talking to, are you?" he added.

"Bar girl, you mean?" she replied, "want to take me out

meester?" She added the last few words mockingly.

This was no bimbo. "Yeah," he said, "not that I'm complaining, I just want to know the score."

She put a hand on his lapel and stroked it. "Relax. I'm strictly freelance." She had a thick husky voice, like black coffee with lots of sugar.

George was thinking, I'm in here, I've struck lucky first shot. He was used to being a bit of a wow with the Far East chicks because of his blond locks (fast thinning unfortunately) but here he was bowling over the Eastern Bloc too! "That's what I like to hear, kid," he said. "I don't know how long I'm going to be staying in this city of yours and it would be nice to know someone, I mean really get to know someone!" He nodded his head at her meaningfully, resisting the impulse to wink and say nudge, nudge.

She carried on looking at him just as coolly, then she laughed. "In the biblical sense, you mean?" She took the first drag he'd seen her take on the cigarette.

My, she was switched on. He went for it. "I was wondering if you'd maybe like to come back to my hotel?" He shrugged, wondering if maybe that was like premature ejaculation, giving away the fact you were pretty desperate for some company. Bad move, he thought, the price had just doubled, but it was only those daft *litas* anyway. The expense account would cover it. Then she removed her shades and he concentrated on her dark eyes but her eyelashes were long and she was looking down as she sipped ever so deliberately at her drink. Then she looked up and her eyes held his and he was suddenly immersed in those deep pools until he realised it was his head that was swimming. And his eye-sight was playing up again: everything was blurred just like it was in immersed too. How had that come on? He'd have to get it checked out. Should he see someone here? Did they even have proper doctors here? Then just as quickly as she'd put on that alluring look she snapped out of it and the shades went back on. "I'll think about it," she said. "Depends what you've got in mind?" It was a bit non-committal, nothing definite, but so far it was no knock back.

George ordered another drink. The place was getting hot and he noticed he was perspiring. He suddenly felt weaker, as if some energy had been drained from him. He could pin it down to that moment of concentration. Just then when he'd looked in her eyes and seen there something as deep and dark as the Siberian mines and he thought he'd seen that look before but nothing like as intense. "What do you think I've got in mind?" he riposted, trying to sound nonchalant. He took out the packet of cigarettes he reserved for occasions like this. The girl smoked so it was a sure-fire winner with her. He only smoked when he was on the razzle or wanted to curry favour. She took the cigarette and drew in deeply after he'd lit it from the Dunhill lighter. "Well?"

he said expectantly. She raised an eyebrow. "I asked you a question." He was feeling cockier now. As if the fact he'd bought her a drink and a smoke gave him rights. She was his now - to some extent at least. She hadn't been forced to accept his largesse.

She stood with that one leg slightly forward from her body and it was amazing how her dress clung to her. It was a provocative pose. She had good legs too, like a dancer's with pronounced but shapely calves and narrow ankles. There was enough thigh on show to suggest musculariyt without overdevelopment. Her manner was still nonchalant, as if she wasn't in deep, she had plenty of time to make up her mind. She pronounced at last: "I think you're after what all men are after, Georgi."

"H yean, and what would that be then?"

She ignored the question. "And I think you think I can provide it."

George was conscious of the barman looking at him, holding his drink. Slightly unnerved by his concentrated stare he took the beer. He noticed a bullnecked man from Zoya's previous entourage also staring at him. Together they made him feel nervous. Nonetheless, he tried to concentrate on the game. "Can you?" he responded.

She smiled, an expert, giving nothing away. "What do

you think?"

He chucked a couple of notes across to the barman. "I think you'd be fantastic!" The shades gave nothing away, but she understood him all right. He looked around nervously as he saw the scrum of men in the far corner edge nearer. "Look, there's a few of your friends in here taking more than a passing interest in us. Maybe we could go somewhere else?"

"No problem," she replied. "Wait here." She went over towards her old group, no doubt to allay their fears about her new consort and it coincided with his suddenly feeling really unwell. Oh no, he thought, not now! It was odd because he was having hot and cold flushes and his eyesight became blurred again, reminding him of his problems at Heathrow, and then, as if some god had just answered his prayer, it just improved again. Whoa! What was that? He thought and he blinked hard, concentrating his mind.

Meanwhile, Zoya seemed to be flitting about on several errands, perhaps saying goodnight to everyone she knew, like she'd hooked the fish and didn't expect to be back. She became locked in conversation with the bullnecked man; they looked over at him a number of times. George licked his lips; they were cracked and dry. There was danger here. He didn't want any trouble with the local hooligans; maybe the man was her pimp and she was covering her tracks?

That reminded him they hadn't talked moolahs. That wasn't like him. He usually got his priorities right. He mopped his brow. Jesus! It was back! He really was feeling weak. It was something to do with the atmosphere in here. For a moment he had a fear of Legionnaire's and then it occurred to him he was the only one showing signs of feeling this way so it must be something to do with fatigue. With a gulp he recalled the plane almost falling from the sky, tossed around like chaff in a whirlwind. He'd ask her about money as soon as she returned; he needed to know the bottom line. It wasn't exactly the spirit of romance but there was no use kidding this was a romantic situation, it was a business transaction. He got something from her, in return for which he gave something - hard currency, U.S dollars he'd bet. None of that funny stuff. He wasn't bothered. That was the way it should be. It was best to start out with all the ground rules clear. He didn't fancy arguing the toss with the Baltic bulldog and it wouldn't look good if his Lithuanian colleagues had to intervene in a local contretemps. His credibility was at stake in this deal until he got the commitment fee in the bag. He hadn't forgotten how he'd nearly screwed up on one in Nigeria because of a slight altercation over a bit of local skirt and Marty wasn't very friendly for a while after that, accusing him of taking his eye off the ball. He couldn't give him that same opportunity this time. There was big money changing hands here.

The Lithuanians thought they were baiting up a sprat to

catch a mackerel but what they didn't know was that a shark was swallowing the sprat. It was ironic, really, that they were approaching it like that because the bank had always said they were looking for a real deal to back, something to clean the more dubious money up with, and the truth was this one looked sound. These Baltic folk were good people. They could make the project work. It was a tried and tested process. It worked in Western Europe. It was just about globalisation, outsourcing. Here they could do it cheaper because of the labour rates and the thing about these guys was they were good workers, industrious and intelligent. They were like the Germans. For ten years anyway they'd get away with that before some other third tier economy usurped them in their turn. So it was a good scheme, as long as they were good managers and there was no reason to think they couldn't suss that too. He'd toyed around with the idea, treating the money like the credibility guarantee. Ultimately his word counted but it wasn't his call and the truth was he knew Marty would scam it. The return wasn't for five years; the bank liked to double its capital in 18 months. Marty was setting up his retirement fund and he was no longer in for the long haul. It was bad timing. Your first profit, that's your best: Marty's motto was all of theirs now.

Still, he liked to kid himself his word counted for more than most and that he could think about it, once the bond was in the bag. Maybe he'd decide how to advise it by how good this chick behaved to him. He tried her

48

with a reprise of his words to the air-hostess as soon as she got back. "I hope you're going to be good to me," he said. "The welfare of a lot of your countrymen is riding on this." He patted her backside gently, leaving her in no doubt what he was talking about. He was pleased to see for the first time, by the way she turned and looked at him even though those now infuriating shades, that he'd got under her skin. It gave him a feeling of power. He felt like a conqueror. She leaned across him and he was momentarily knocked out by the twin assault of her perfume and cleavage. "You don't get many of them to the pound," he tried to joke and then noticed his words hadn't come out right, he'd sort of slurred them. What was happening to him? He shook his head, sure it went back to when he'd looked into those dark Slavonic eyes. He looked at his glass. Was this the strong stuff?

She helped him as he staggered slightly. "Come on, let's get you back to your hotel." Partly leaning on her he negotiated the staircase with difficulty. He'd never got drunk so quickly. What did they put in that brew? They headed for the corner miles away. It took ages to navigate. It was like the buildings were part of the wall of a bouncy castle; they never stayed still and it felt like treading rubber underfoot. There seemed to be hundreds of people milling round, the nightclubs coming out and everyone congregating in the open air. He remembered he still hadn't talked about the wages of sin. He had to do that. He kept on reminding himself but every time the thought came his mouth seemed to blather on about something totally different as if he couldn't bring himself to raise the subject. I'm not getting sentimental, am I? He thought. But no, he knew he had to get to the bottom line. Everything was too fluid. There was room for misunderstanding. He found himself walking with a sort of matelot-type motion, from side to side as if on a rolling deck. The cobbled streets seemed to bend like a rope bridge in the wind. He remembered the walk down from the hotel and groaned inwardly when he thought he had to repeat it. "Have you ever done it on cocaine?" she said, "it makes a difference."

Cocaine, cocaine? Had someone slipped him a mickey? But he'd never felt like this on coke! "Is there no way you can get a taxi in this dump?" He was amazed by the whining, self-pitying sound of his own voice. As if in answer a vehicle chugged slowly up the cobbled street, one of its front lights out. It emerged from the shadows, and it was the battered old Trabant, its one weak headlight picking them out unerringly. "Bloody hell, it's Tomas's man!" he said. "He's some frigging use after all!"

He was laughing. It was all too amusing for words. He made a great show of flagging down the car, standing in the middle of the road with a militaristic, Hitlerian posture, doing the straight arm with the right and the moustache with the left. The vehicle groaned to a halt and he bowed, or rather bent double in what he thought was a courtly gesture, and held the door open for Zoya. He gave her backside one hell of a squeeze as he helped her in. It felt good and firm and he was looking forward to snuggling up against that. She seemed to feel the same by the way she giggled as she clambered on to the rear seat, no longer offended by his effrontery.

He climbed in and sat down next to her and found himself suddenly necking with her, her tongue in his mouth, her limbs restless, his hands squeezing her slender waist as if they wanted to meet around it. He pulled away to allow her to undo the top button of his shirt. Were they going to do it in the car? He couldn't help but take a look at the driver but he was taciturn, ramrod straight at the wheel, looking straight ahead like all good chauffeurs should. "That's right," he said, unable to hide the glee in his voice, "eyes front," and then he found himself once again looking into those dark, liquid eyes and there was something familiar in there, a look perhaps, an expression, but it was too long ago and he didn't really want to know. She had the shades off now, the first of the apparel to go, the first of many when he got her back to his place. This one could stay the night; he liked to kick them out normally after doing the business but Zoya, if that was her real name, was one to wake up next to.

Moments later his head slumped and through the darkness he could hear the drone of the engine. It went on for a long time. "Good," he muttered, although he wasn't sure why. He never did raise the cash issue.

CHAPTER 5

The angel battered down on him, its claws knotted around the pounding hammer. In the background the fire still burned beneath the trees with its grisly sacrifice. The angel's dark and leathery wings provided a canopy. His arms stretched up to it above his head. Dark swirling water dragged him into a vortex. Slowly he started to surface. He came to and looked about him groggily. He was immersed in a bath of cold water. Had he climbed in and fallen asleep? The door was open; through it he could see the bed was wrecked as if it had seen some hectic action. How come he couldn't remember that? It wasn't like him to forget a hot session. His mind went back to Zoya and the overriding impression of her dark glasses. Wow! he thought. You'd think I'd remember shagging that!

His hands were stretched out behind his head; he couldn't move them. He craned backwards but his head was like a lump of lead. Despite the reluctance of his neck muscles he twisted it round sufficiently to see they were attached to the tap by thin cord. He shuddered when he thought that, if they hadn't been tied, his head wouldn't have been kept out of the water. He would have drowned! It was a horrible thought but what had happened to him? The dark angel was still hammering, the thumping and the noise outside his head. He could hear shouting too. Dimly it all came back. Where was the woman? His eyes swivelled feverishly. They felt as if they were out on stalks, seeing things in a sort of circular motion. There was someone at the door but it was miles away, as if he was seeing it through a telescope. Then, with a jolt, he remembered his briefcase. They mustn't get that! His whole game plan would be blown! Necessity forced its way through the grogginess and he shouted out. "Help!" What would whoever it was think when they saw him like this? It didn't matter. He had to check his briefcase was still there.

The door opened; Tomas walked gingerly in, followed by an anxious looking manager and then the porter. Tomas spied him through the open bathroom door. "George," he exclaimed, but his voice sounded disembodied and gravelly as if it were being sifted through charcoal, "what have you been doing? I've been trying to wake you for ages. I've knocked and telephoned. I had to bring the manager. We had to use the master key." He said it all as if he was berating George for the trouble he had been put to but then broke off and looked aghast as he realised George was actually tied up in the bath. "What happened?" he shouted. He uttered some words in Lithuanian to the manager who came in and looked perplexed. The hotel porter had a sardonic smile on his face. "My briefcase," George croaked, "is it in the wardrobe?"

The porter started undoing the bonds and found the

knots too tight so he went away to get a knife. Tomas checked the wardrobe and came back with the briefcase. "What's the combination?" he said, "I'll check everything's there."

"No! If it's still locked it's okay," George replied. The porter came back and finally succeeded in cutting the Gordian Knot and he felt the circulation begin to come back into his wrists. There was a searing pain as it did so.

"How did this happen?" Tomas asked. George tried to get up. The porter had to help him. He grabbed a towel and put it round himself. He staggered back into the bedroom and slumped on the bed. "I don't know," he moaned. "I'm ill."

"He came in with woman last night," the porter said in English. George thought, fucking grass! He didn't need it rubbed into the Lithuanian contingent that he'd been out whoring. But no doubt Vytautus would have reported back anyway.

Disapproving clucking noises followed. He decided, if his cover was blown, best not to try and duck the issue. "Yeah, she was called Zoya, what happened to her?" The sound echoed round his head as if he was talking underwater.

The porter shrugged, his English just about shot. "He didn't see the woman leave, "Tomas translated.

"I'll bet he didn't," he groaned. "Conveniently!"

"Oh no, George, I can assure you that the night porter at this prestigious hotel would not be telling lies."

"Oh no? He's not likely to have taken a backhander, you don't think!"

Tomas either didn't get or chose to ignore the sarcasm. "Have you checked your things, has anything been stolen?"

"I don't know," George groaned. To satisfy their curiosity he struggled across to his jacket. His wallet was intact. His cash was there, his credit cards, his watch. "All present and correct," he drawled in a thick voice. He looked up at them and caught the contempt in their eyes. He was just another drunken, western businessman. That's what they thought. He wanted to say it's not like that but it wouldn't do any good because, in their eyes, it was and their eyes were probably right. Cocaine, the girl had mentioned cocaine! Best not mention that. God knows what happened if you admitted drug use. But the thought of it made him want to go to the loo. "'Scuse me," he said and he stumbled towards the bathroom. He made as if to pee and then he saw floating in the john a number of used condoms, pink in colour. "Jesus!" he shouted, "it must have been a hell of a night!"

Hearing the shout and thinking something was wrong Tomas ran in. He pulled up, looking at George and he started to apologise. Then his eyes followed the stream of urine to the pan and he clocked the condoms. He glared back at George, embarrassed now as if he'd been let down, and retired from the room. George stared in disbelief at the ceiling as he heard him outside, furtively speaking to the manager. There was no doubting what their opinion of him would be when he emerged. Shit! It was unfair. He hadn't performed like that since he was twenty or so and he couldn't remember a bloody thing! But what about Zoya? What a woman! "Hey, Tomas!" he shouted, "that gorilla of yours, the driver guy, whatever his name is, he brought us back here. He'll know the girl."

"Really?" Tomas repeated. "But that is too bad. He's gone on vacation today. I can't contact him."

"Very convenient!" George muttered. He kicked the bathroom door shut. He studied his grizzled face in the mirror. The mornings weren't kind to him anymore. He shaved with some difficulty and brushed his teeth. Then he stepped back outside. The manager was shaking his head. The porter was tut-tutting. Tomas was trying to smooth things over. He turned to George. "We are at least an hour late for the meeting."

He thought his head was clearing and he replied, "okay, give me twenty minutes to get showered and dressed, and then we'll go."

"Are you sure?" Tomas replied, "Can you cope with it?"

"I'll feel better after a shower," George replied. "Look Tomas, I haven't got the slightest idea what went on here last night. Your guess is as good as mine."

"Maybe you drank too much alcohol?"

"Bollocks, I had three pints, maybe four, of that draught lager, it's not the strongest stuff I've ever had."

Tomas shook his head. "Three pints of the local beer should not leave you like that," he said in his precise, effeminate tones.

"Yeah, that's what I figured," George replied, "so either I had a bad pint or someone slipped me a mickey."

"A mickey?" Tomas looked perplexed. He had blue, stary eyes when he looked perplexed, three o'clock half struck. But he was quite captivated by those blue eyes and the look in them. It could be quite intense and George was struggling for the comparisons, which he put down to the fact that he didn't have an artistic mind.

George groaned. "A mickey finn, a spikey gin! A drink laced with drugs!" He just about refrained from adding the 'moron' on the end.

Tomas was beside himself at the thought that his countrymen could behave so despicably to a revered guest. "But who would do such a thing? Maybe the girl? But you said nothing is missing." He shrugged as if it were an inexplicable mystery. It was strange. The woman had taken nothing from him! He must have been helpless. She'd tied him up in the bath but taken nothing from him! Why had she put him in it? To try and revive him? Did she think he'd suffered a stroke or something? A regular Florence Nightingale! But how had she put him in it? He was no featherweight. "You could report it to the police," Tomas added, "but what will you tell them?"

"Well, what happened?"

"You mean, this girl came back to your place and gave you a good time and then she left, taking....? I mean it doesn't even look as if she accepted any payment?" George opened his hands and looked at Thomas, who shook his head, which was the cue for the manager and porter to excuse themselves. As soon as they got out into the corridor, with the door safely shut behind them but not quite as soundproofed as they thought, they burst into laughter.

George clapped Tomas on the shoulder and received a nervous grin by way of response. "I'll be okay. Must be getting on a bit, that's all, can't take it anymore." In his heart, he knew the explanation wasn't that simple but he insisted on walking the half mile or so to Tomas's office in the hope that would put the spring back in his step. It was a mistake because, by the time they got there, he felt as if he was about to be sick. The shower hadn't freshened him up as he'd hoped, neither had the autumnal feel in the air.

He managed an hour of the meeting and then cracked up. Waves of nausea swept over him. Tomas explained the situation to his colleagues, taking care to leave out the more sensitive parts. George felt like the grinning idiot in the background, trying to shrug it off. But the businessmen were sympathetic. Someone even suggested food poisoning. "You should take him to the hospital," he added.

Tomas decided this was a good idea and, in spite of George's protests, he finally persuaded him. "You have insurance?" he asked.

"Oh, yeah, sure," George replied, wondering vaguely if his secretary had fixed any up.

"Maybe I was wrong. Maybe you should also be talking to the police?" Tomas added.

"What for?"

"About this woman. Maybe she did something to you?"

"Well, it certainly looks like she did something to me, but I suspect it's no more illegal here than anywhere else." Tomas grimaced. Even in his slightly befuddled state George could see that his patriotic pride was offended by the thought that he, a foreigner, had used one of Lithuania's young women for carnal purposes. "Oh, grow up, Tomas!" he exclaimed. "Look at me, do I look like I came out of it best?"

At the hospital he was put into a cubicle where he waited with Tomas for the doctor, who turned out to be in his mid-forties, quite tall, fair with a moustache and an English speaker. "I did part of my training in Liverpool," he explained.

"Scouser, eh?" George replied. He managed a grin even though it felt as if he needed the assistance of several pulleys to make his lips move.

"Yes. Like the Beatles, eh, and Kenny Dalglish!" the doctor replied.

"Don't I know you, Doctor?" Tomas intervened, his voice full of excitement. The doctor turned to study him, a puzzled look on his face. "I'm sure I have met you," Tomas added, still speaking in English for George's benefit. "You lit the bonfire at the television tower! I was there!"

"Well," the doctor replied, "that was a long time ago."

"My God!" Tomas replied, "But we sent such a message to Moscow, did we not?"

The doctor still had the same puzzled look in his eyes as he returned the young man's rapt gaze. "Yes, I suppose we did." They still spoke in English for his benefit and George's mouth had fallen open as he listened to Tomas. It occurred to him that he spoke of these things to increase his standing with his English associate.

"I was there!" Tomas continued, still full of childish enthusiasm. "I was there too when I saw the tanks roll out. I counted them, 20, 30, 40, 50. I thought how different it could have been. How they could have been rolling in the opposite direction, just as they did in Hungary, in Czechoslovakia!" He was in full flow now, reliving the memory while the doctor looked on indulgently and George did the mental equivalent of star jumps in the corner. They should be paying attention to him! "I looked into those tanks. There was only one with a defiant Hammer and Sickle flying but I tell you those eyes, those eyes from inside those dark, dark turrets. Some were just glad to be leaving, they were like rabbits' eyes but some ….." He paused, the memory of the moment overpowering his gift for language. "Some were like rats' eyes, so full of malice, as if they wanted to turn their guns on us there and then. But they couldn't. Their turrets were turned forty five degrees away. They couldn't. We had won."

The doctor smiled, his eyebrows raised. "Finished?" he asked and he turned back to George. "Sorry, my friend," he said, "you must excuse our enthusiasm for democracy. It has come as a great surprise to us after so long in a wilderness." He began methodically to examine his patient, taking his blood pressure, then a blood sample. Before he inserted the syringe, he said almost nonchalantly, "have you ever tested positive for AIDS or HIV?"

George looked suspiciously at the needle. "Not up to now, no," he replied.

The doctor laughed. "No problem," he said, "all hygienic, very sanitised."

"That makes me feel really good." He had a horror of needles.

After the ordeal was over he was sent down the corridor for an ECG. The old girl working the electrodes didn't even speak, let alone in his language, just grunting in short, commanding sounds which were unintelligible except for the accompanying pointing. She looked like the typical Russian housewife of popular myth, big, brooding and monosyllabic. He stared at all the electronic gear which looked prehistoric and said, "excuse me, are you sure this isn't the electric chair? " He was alarmed at the sudden thought that he could be electrocuted by a loose connection - who would know? They'd just cover it up! He sat up on the cot and she slapped him back down with a straight arm clothesline. His rib cage reverberated with the shock. How do they treat the healthy ones he thought, but he smiled obsequiously as she turned and glowered, reading his mind. When she let him up, a wheelchair was waiting for him. "What the f....!" he started to exclaim but his voice trailed off as the big woman lifted him bodily off the stretcher, slammed him into the chair and began pushing him silently, except for the squeak of the wheels, down the long corridors where the light seemed to die a horrible death, a few of the fittings still twitching in their final throes. They flickered on and off, accompanied by a horrible, shorting sound. "Don't you have a national grid here?" he complained, squinting into the darkness. He tried to get out of the chair but a hand firmly clamped his shoulder, just about cracking the clavicle. "Jesus, Ludmilla! What were you, Olympic shot put champion?"

"You sit still please," she said in broken English, proving she had some. It was the most she had uttered since the tests began and it didn't sound like a request, it sounded like sit there or I'll nail your ass to the seat! Then a young nurse took over from her and pushed him towards a lift. He was pleased with the change. She was a tasty looking blond and her tunic was slightly open above the midriff, showing creamy white skin and a hint of bra. He was thinking she'd do to tuck him in but just as he'd begun to enjoy this reverie a bewildered Tomas appeared from a side passage and trotted along by his side. George felt like saying, trust you to show up like a wet fart when I'm starting to think life might not be so bad after all, even in a Russian infirmary, but he was still reliant on this deal so instead he asked, "how's it gannin, Tomas?"

"Gannin?" The perplexed look was back.

George sighed. "Going! I meant how are things going? What have you heard about me?"

"Just precautions," Tomas said. "Your blood pressure is very low, your pulse is slow, they want to keep you in tonight for observations." He spoke in that precise, clipped but effeminate way which George had grown accustomed to.

How did he service his Mrs? He sounded such a wuss. "My pulse is always slow and my blood pressure's always low!" George replied irritably.

"Yes, well the way they're describing it, you're one notch up from dead," Tomas retorted, exhibiting a knack for irony which George hadn't guessed he possessed. "What happened to you, George?" Tomas went on, "this woman gave you something more than you bargained for!"

Did he have a little gleam in his eye, as if he was enjoying this modern fable? "I keep telling you, I don't know," George replied. "What time do I get out?"

"They want you to stay overnight at least."

"You can't be serious! We've got a deal to do. I can't
be hanging about in a hospital. There are mountains to
move, kid!" Tomas shrugged. It wasn't his decision.
There was nothing he could do about it. George thought
for a moment. No way did he want to delay this deal.
He had to get that letter of credit through. Then he had
a brainwave. "Okay, you bring the guys to the hospital
room, we'll finish the meeting there."

"The doctor says not today," Tomas replied in best, wet
blanket fashion.

George breathed out loudly in frustration. The nurse
pushed the wheelchair into a spacious twin room. The
gap opened even further as she shifted position and now
he got a view of her navel. George's mouth dropped
open. She noticed and ever so demurely did up the
loose button. "Spoilsport!" George quipped. She had no
English but grinned impishly so she understood all
right. George pressed Tomas to translate but whatever
he said made no impression so George figured he'd
bottled it. He had to content himself with the look he
got at her backside as she bent over the bed. His parts
were still in working order, that at least was a relief. So
was the fact he was the only occupant of the room.
He'd had a dread of lying in a ward surrounded by
Baltic false teeth and wooden legs.

As if on cue, the Liverpool doctor put his head round
the door. The disembodied head with the big, slightly
unnecessary grin made him look like a cartoon

character. "This is a KGB room," he said.

"Come again?" George replied.

"It's the room visiting KGB bigwigs used if they were hospitalised here," the doc went on - he really had picked up a Scouse accent. "Of course there isn't any KGB anymore so we reserve it for VIP guests. Like yourself."

George grinned, suitably flattered. His surroundings weren't plush. They weren't uncomfortable but Spartan was the best way to describe them. The toilet was positively agricultural but as hospitals went it could be worse. He'd once had hepatitis in Nigeria. Now that was a bastard! Pneumonia in Hong Kong? No, that was pretty comfortable: not the pneumonia, the hospital. When he came to consider the geography of his indispositions he realised he'd been ill in some out of the way places, which just showed how much he got around because he was hard to knock out of sync. He could start an adventure travel club based on the hospitals he'd visited. But this was the only place where you couldn't remember getting laid until you woke up in the KGB ward.

He didn't like the look of it either when they fixed up the drip over his bed. "Do I need that?" he asked. The Scouser shrugged sympathetically. The bottles weren't the modern plastic type. They were large and made of glass, Victoriana. "Did they come as a job lot from the

Crimean War?" he added much to the doc's amusement.

The nurse came and pumped up his arm. Even so she had ten or so shots before she found a vein. The inside of his elbow was black and blue by the time she'd finished. "Hey, I hope you take an injection better than you give one," he quipped, unable to disguise entirely the leer.

He looked beseechingly at the Scouser, who shrugged. "They're better at it than we are," he said as if that was some consolation.

Tomas sat and talked with him for a time. He was trying to get a few details about the deal clear in his own head before he held further talks with his board. He agreed he would try and bring his colleagues the next day and they would hold the meeting there if George was going to be hospitalised any longer. He asked if George wanted him to take his notes away and type them up but he refused. Tomas looked at him strangely, probably noticing yet again the way he kept hold of the briefcase. George realised it must have looked odd. He had to be careful. This wasn't long ago a land of secret police and sudden disappearances during the night. It had been ingrained in the population to notice anything suspicious.

Then Tomas went and George realised how lousy he felt. He tried to read a thriller but he couldn't get into it.

He wasn't much of a reader anyway. He was an action man and the sort of action they had in thrillers was usually either too incredible or too tame. The night nurse came and changed his drip. She wasn't as heavy handed as the day nurse and he thanked her. She didn't have quite the buxom beauty either so he didn't josh with her. He ate a little semolina and drank a lot of water. The night nurse said the night doctor would come and see him. "The night doctor?" he responded. Apparently it was her night off but she always came in anyway, late on, just for an hour, to check there were no emergencies. "Regular Florence Nightingale," he said, remembering he'd thought the same of Zoya's putting him in the bath (if she did, and if she didn't he definitely didn't want to go there) but in a slightly more cynical way. She was probably like the weight-lifter who ran the torture unit downstairs which masqueraded as an ECG room.

He stayed awake as long as he could but the drug they'd given him made it difficult to keep his eyes open. He dozed off into a heavy sleep. It was strange. He dreaded dreaming again of the angel. It was becoming too frequent an occupant of his sleeping life and there was that thing again of a creature burning in the hard wood and it looked like a man. Then the creature and the sacrifice disappeared into the darkness and, instead, he dreamt of Zoya. She came along in a white coat dressed just like the Scouser and looked down at him. She was speaking to him. "How are you feeling?"

"What did you do to me? Was it cocaine?"

She laughed in that way that Zoya had laughed at him, very dismissive, very superior. He'd liked that, he remembered. "Cocaine?" she said. "Do you think cocaine would have that effect?" She shook her head slowly. It was a magnificent head. She wasn't a whore; she was a strong woman.

Dressed now in the doctor's smock she looked even more enticing than the night before. She was different, much more relaxed. The old Zoya had given him a powerful sense of his own inferiority. The dream one had nothing to prove. He was thinking he'd like to grab hold of her in his dream. You can, he was telling himself but somehow it was taboo. You didn't behave that way with a doctor. She might do something nasty to you, like give you a lethal injection or just a dose of some foul-tasting medicine - just because she could. Still, he'd really like to give her one.

It was then she laughed as if she knew exactly what he was thinking. He heard the door open and sat up. He saw a white coat disappear as the door shut. He burst out in perspiration. It wasn't a dream.

CHAPTER 6

Next morning Tomas visited again and seemed to be in a good mood about something. He'd enquired of the doctor about holding the Board Meeting in the hospital room and it was okay as long as it didn't go on too long and wasn't stressful. "How do you feel about it?"

George still felt weak. He still had no idea what had caused his relapse but the most oppressive symptom was a feeling of other worldliness, as if he wasn't quite there, his mind and body somehow separate entities. The one could contemplate the other but dispassionately, as if it were no part of him. He had suffered viral pneumonia once when in the Far East and that was the nearest feeling he could liken it to. He shuddered when he thought that time he'd been near death. Still, he wasn't dead. He was here. No use looking back, there were worlds to conquer, deals to do. "I'll manage," he said with a martyred voice. "I've got to be back in London in three days. I've got a meeting to chair."

"About this loan?"

George couldn't help swinging the haymaker, just to up the ante. "Nah," he exclaimed dismissively, "that's a really big deal!" He made it sound as if this ten million was really small potatoes, the home grown variety. Tomas wasn't however phased by the put down. His smooth, soft face still wore the same self-satisfied smirk. George wondered if he wore make up or some kind of cream - if he did he should change beauty counsellor, because he was a good looking lad, he didn't need gunge. With a hint of jealousy, George looked in his myopic way at his thick, luxuriant head of fair hair, a bit bushy for his taste, but he had to admit the lad would equally suit a skinhead with chiselled features like his and those high cheekbones. He was like that Irish singer. What was her name? Sinead O'Connor. He had a sudden feeling of *déjà vu* but he couldn't remotely understand why. Did Tomas look different today? Did he know something George didn't know?

He found the smirk on Tomas's face a trifle irksome but nonetheless found himself mitigating his own insult. "Don't you worry about this loan, bonny lad," he added, reverting to the Geordie roots he often tried to hide in the sophisticated world of investment banking but which drew him back whenever his confidence was at its nadir, "when the deal's done the money's as good as on the table. It'll just come plummeting out of the sky." He pointed and looked upward as if to demonstrate the trajectory of the falling loot.

Tomas's eyes followed his hand signals and he gazed expectantly at the heavens. George tried to laugh. It came out as a bit of a croak. "You get all the players

together this afternoon and we'll try and put it to bed."
He cleared his throat and this time was more successful
as he forced a laugh at his own pun. He was reflective
for a moment then he thought it was best confronting
the issue head on. Tomas's reserve no doubt was
derived from his lack of appreciation of George's moral
standards. "You know I met that woman the other
night?" It sounded almost like a confessional. Tomas
looked at the ground. George noticed the long eyelashes
and wondered, not for the first time, if he batted for the
other side. It was troubling because he found the
younger man strangely beguiling. He'd never
considered himself a queer but the things some of the
lads who'd gone away - gone to prison that is - had said
rang true. Maybe even he wouldn't be so choosey after
a while. Any port in a storm, so to speak. If it had
happened to them, big lads, bench pressers, it could
happen to anyone. George mixed with people like that.
He kept it separate from his business life in one sense,
i.e they never came to his office, but he was the fixer,
he had to know those people because sometimes you
needed to use gorillas. Still, he was glad he'd never had
to resort to it. He turned his attention back to Tomas as
he replied.

"I know," Tomas said - almost shyly, as if he didn't
really want to discuss it.

"Oh come on Tomas, don't act like you're wet behind
the ears," George pressed him, "you're a married man
now, so you must have found out about the birds and

the bees?"

"The birds and the bees?"

He'd lost Tomas off. "Yeah, what men and women do together. You know, where the babies come from when there aren't enough storks to go round!" The younger man looked even more uncomfortable with his blunt approach. "It can't be a total surprise to you that I pulled a woman at the Indigo. It just happened. That's the way it is sometimes." Tomas nodded, waiting for him to continue. "I know you don't like it that foreigners come here and, just because they've got a fat wallet, they can pick up your chicks, but that's life. That's the way it's been for centuries. I didn't ask to be put in that situation but we have a saying in England that you never look a gift horse in the mouth. Okay? Capisce?" Tomas nodded again but it was noticeable he wasn't contributing to the conversation so George came to the point. "Anyway," he said, "whatever the ins and outs of that situation, something crazy happened last night."

"Last night?"

"Here. In the hospital." Now Tomas showed interest, inclining his head slightly, his mouth clamped shut. His eyes never left George's. "Yeah, the night doctor came in and well." He hesitated. "Look, I know this is going to sound crazy, but I'd swear it was the same girl."

"The same girl?" Tomas looked perplexed. His blue, staring eyes rolled in horror.

"You know," George replied, holding his hands up for emphasis, "the girl I met in the bar, Zoya."

Tomas grinned and it was like a lot of pulleys had to work together to get that horrified smirk back on his face. "Are you saying," he replied slowly and in a way that George might have thought of as menacing if he'd concentrated, "that the girl you picked up in a sleazy night club is a doctor here in the hospital?"

George shrugged. "Yeah," he said at length. "I was very drowsy, but she was standing there large as life. At first I thought I was dreaming but then we had a conversation -"

" - in English?"

"No, stupid, in Swahili!"

Tomas didn't flinch at the insult. "So the woman you picked up in this joint, the whore you picked up, is not only a doctor but she is so fluent in English she had a conversation with you in the middle of the night?" George nodded, his mouth puffed out in acknowledgment of the absurdity of the whole thing. "This is impossible," Tomas snapped, plainly angry.

"Well, impossible or not, it happened. You know what

they say. Eliminate the impossible and what you have left is the truth?"

"You must have been dreaming. Your head is still in a funny state from what happened. You imagined it."

It was George's turn to grow angrier. "Are you listening to me you dickhead, I told you at first I thought that but then I realised I was wide awake. And she was standing right there. Where you are now."

"And I suppose she was dressed like a whore? Just for you!" Tomas was extracting the Michael now.

"No! Did I say that? Watch my lips. She was dressed like a doctor. White coat, stethoscope, the lot."

"But George, you know how it is with fever! Sometimes you can think you are awake when you aren't, you can dream you are awake...."

"I was not fucking asleep godammit!"

"I am sure the night doctor is not this Zoya."

"Oh, you're sure, are you? Well, maybe it's just her alias, or her professional name?"

"Professional name? I don't understand."

"You know, the name she uses when she's whoring.

Wouldn't be right to use the name she reserves for the Florence Nightingale bit." George rather enjoyed seeing Tomas wince.

"I think not, and I do not want you spreading these rumours about the night doctor because it could get her a bad reputation."

"You don't say! She'd be front page news in the tabloids back home. Sexy doctor takes a shot. She gives one too and it sure packs a punch. My head's still aching and it's thirty six hours ago. Think about it, though! Maybe the Lithuanian National Health doesn't pay enough. I wonder if we ask her nicely she'll come back and give me a blow job?" He could see that Tomas was at the end of his tether and he was enjoying winding him up. He was so bloody precious. "I think she might you know. I didn't hold any secrets back from her, I explained I was pretty well endowed - "he winked at Tomas - "and judging by the way she wrecked my bed she couldn't get enough. Didn't charge me either! That's gratitude for you!"

Tomas looked exasperated. "How many times do I have to tell you *that woman* wasn't one of our doctors?"

"Our doctors? The female medical staff aren't allowed to get one up them, aren't they? What does it do? Make their hands shake? All I can say is, that nurse must get plenty, judging by the way she sticks the needle in." He held out his arm and winced. "Look at that!" He showed where the inside of the elbow was almost black from the bruising.

Tomas was so angry with George he waved him away and turned his back, standing over by the window and staring out. It was four floors to the ground and he looked as if he was thinking of chucking George through it. The patient laughed at his discomfort. He'd had just about enough of this tin pot country. All he wanted to do was work the scam and get out of here. What with this shithole of a hospital and Tomas's pathetic patriotism? You'd think every Lithuanian child was a virgin birth the way he went on. He'd like to meet his wife, see what she thought of having a wimp like him around. He'd short show her what a real man was, although when he thought about it she'd probably be exactly the same sort as Tomas. Who else would marry a fairy?

Before the silence could become too embarrassing the Scouser appeared. "Well, if it ain't me old mate the Scouse," George said affably holding out his hand to shake the doctor's.

"No mention of this, please," Tomas implored as the doctor made a point of reading George's notes.

Tomas's entreaties had no effect on him. Just for the hell of it he was going to ask who the night tart was but the doctor took the wind out of both their sails and told him, "my colleague Dr. Juska told me you had terrible troubles last night. Bad nightmares." He leaned over and felt his forehead.

"Have I met this Dr. Juska?" George asked, winking at Tomas who looked distinctly pissed off.

"You did last night. She told me you had a long conversation."

George made victory noises, holding a hand to his mouth and pumping the other as if playing a trombone. The doctor looked at him askance, not appreciating the triumphant noises were not aimed at him. Tomas's face, meanwhile, betrayed his annoyance. "Sure, we had a conversation, but I was sleepy at the time and I couldn't take it all in. I'd like to meet her again."

The Scouser drew the figure of the perfect woman in the air. "I don't blame you, and she's single too. Eat your heart out!"

"You've been there, doc, have you?"

The doctor looked horrified. "No, but…."

"I know. You'd like to be!" The two of them roared with laughter while Tomas stood seething. "Lighten up, Tomas," George said. "It's only a bit crack, man." He turned back to the doctor. "So I'll meet her tonight? Or am I going out now?"

"I'm not sure," he said, "I haven't had all the tests back yet, but, no, you won't be meeting Zoya tonight, she's finished this week's shift and she won't be back on until next week."

Both Tomas and George were staring at him open-mouthed. "Did you say Zoya?" George asked.

"Yes," he said, puzzled by George's reaction, "she is called Zoya." Tomas was just about demented. He had to turn to the window again to hide his anger.

"Then I've got to see her again," George said. "I won't be right until I see her again. Only she knows what happened to me."

The doctor looked perplexed. "What do you mean?" Tomas was making secret signs to George not to take the matter further. The doctor turned to him, visibly annoyed. "Would you mind leaving us, so I can examine the patient?"

Tomas departed in a fit of pique. The doctor carried out a formal examination. He made George touch the end of his nose with his forefinger, his eyes shut, stand on one leg. He turned him around and made him open his eyes and walk. "You aren't quite right yet," he concluded, "but you'll do."

"That's a bit of a change," George replied, puzzled.

The doc ignored that but took hold of George's right arm and turned the hand so that the inside of the wrist was showing. "What's that?" He was referring to the graze which bisected the limb from ulna to radius.

George looked at it puzzled. It was the merest of scratches. That might be why he'd not noticed it earlier. "Search me," he said.

"There's one on your other arm as well," the Scouser added, turning the left arm over and revealing the elongated cut, as if someone had traced a sharp instrument along it.

George, even more surprised, looked at it closely. The doc was right: the wound was equally slight but it was there. "They are relatively new scratches," the doctor said, "and small enough to have been missed yesterday in your initial examination if you didn't draw them to anyone's attention." George shook his head. He hadn't, because he didn't know they were there. The next question took him totally by surprise. "Have you ever displayed suicidal tendencies?"

"You must be joking! Me? I've got everything to live for!"

The Scouser looked sceptical. "Were you suffering from anything when you came to Lithuania?" George shook his head. "Any stress, any psychological problems?"

George thought about it. "No," he said, "unless..." His voice trailed off.

"Unless what?"

"Well, the flight was funny. There was a time I thought we were going to crash." The Scouser looked interested and indicated to him to say more. "Well, we nearly dropped out of the sky, things were that bad. Then there was the dream."

"The dream?"

"Yeah, I dreamt it again last night."

"Tell me about the dream." He started to write notes on the pad resting on his knee.

George explained about the apparition he'd seen in the dream. "It called itself the angel."

"Do you know anything of Lithuanian mythology?" the doctor asked as he wrote assiduously.

"Are you kidding me?" George shook his head.

"Strange, because what you have described sounds very similar to the god Perkunas. He is the god of the storm in the Baltic pantheon. He is not unlike Thor but has also the attributes of Odin in Scandinavian mythology."

"Oh yeah? Sounds like a regular big shot!"

"Particularly the black creatures remind me of him. These are typical sacrifices to that deity. We Lithuanians kept our heathen traditions much longer than the other Aryan races of Europe."

"Is that a fact now? Well, I know nowt of your traditions, heathen or otherwise so how could I be dreaming of this god?"

"No? Then I am not sure."

"There was the air-stewardess."

"Oh?"

"Yeah, she was telling me stories about Lithuania, you know because the flight was a bit scary. Maybe she mentioned it?"

"Oh, perhaps that will explain it. You will be pleased to know, though, it is good to be visited by this god."

George perked up at that. "Oh, okay!"

"Yes. He is a symbol of courage and success. The top of the world!"

"You don't say! And there's me thinking you must be

barking up the wrong tree! Sorry! No pun intended."

"The tree was an oak, yes?"

"Yeah, that's way I remember it."

"Okay, and a lime?"

"So the dream said." George looked perplexed. "Is there some significance in that?"

The doctor put down his pen. "Well, the oak is a sacred tree here. It is traditionally regarded as male, just as the lime is traditionally regarded as female." He pondered a while. "Interesting! Did you have any specific problems on your mind when you came to Lithuania, before you boarded the aircraft?"

That he was about to cheat them? Should he mention that? No, perhaps that wouldn't be a good idea. Anyway, he didn't see it as a problem. It never had been before. It was just business. Maybe there was one other thing. "Does divorce count?" he asked.

"Most certainly it could."

George decided to give the doctor chapter and verse about his messy separation, which was speedily becoming terminal. All the result of his philandering. The casual observer might have thought he took a grim delight in that. "Do you have any children?" the doctor asked.

"Two. Both pretty well grown up now. They still live at home. With my wife, that is. Soon to be ex-wife." He grimaced as he said that and there was no doubt the doctor noticed because he penned something on the pad. George couldn't help it, though. He tried to hide it but he hadn't got used to it. He and Jen had been an item for a long time.

"How do you get on with them, the children that is?"

"I don't. It's that kind of relationship where I send them greetings cards with cash in. They tear up the bloody cards and send them back."

"What about the cash?"

"Oh, bollocks, they keep that. They're not that stupid."

The doctor saw the funny side. He asked, "Was this very traumatic, this marriage break up?"

"Well, shit no, it was just your average marriage break up."

The doc gave him the eyes as if to say, help me here.

"Well, yeah, we'd been together a long time. But I'm a bit like Bill Clinton you know."

"Bill Clinton? You mean the American president?"

"Yeah. I like women. I can't keep my hands off them, and another piece of my anatomy has difficulty not showing its appreciation when they're around."

"That's very frank."

"My name's George."

The doc laughed. "Okay, Georgi. And you didn't do anything about this?"

"What was I supposed to do? Cut it off? Impossible, marra! I mean, the job I do, millionaire status, there was fanny flying all round the place just daring you to give it six nowt. I mean what is our function?"

"Our function?"

"Yeah, propagation of the species! If you're half a man you'll be there! You know what I mean?"

The doctor had a twinkle in his blue eyes as he listened. "No," he said, "tell me."

"Could this have any bearing?"

"It might, yes."

"You're not going to tell me I invented all this, are you?

Everything that happened to me?"

"Invented it?" The doc looked puzzled.

"You know, imagined it? Like a loony tune."

"No, of course not Georgi."

Funny, George thought, that's the second time he called me that. I didn't tell him she called me Georgi.

If the doctor had noticed anything he gave no sign and he covered over his mistake smoothly. "I'm not going to tell you anything of the sort, but I need to know why you behaved so badly, why you were so affected by what you say was harmless alcohol. The beer here is not strong."

Hmm, George thought. Best not mention the cocaine. The cops'll probably lock me up if I mention that. He wasn't one hundred per cent convinced about these former Soviet countries. Like Tomas had said, old habits die hard. And not just in the corruption stakes, but also in who's working for the State, for the ex-KGB. "Well," he said, "it's not behaving badly in my book, it's natural. It's more than that. It's like you have to do it to prove you're alive. It feels like that. The only time you're really sure you're alive is when you're in bed with a woman." He shrugged. "That's how it is. With me anyway."

"And afterwards?"

"Afterwards? What do you mean afterwards?"

"How do you feel then?"

"Well, usually I just kick them out of bed, don't I? Naff off, whore, no point in keeping someone hanging round you don't like when you've had your end away!"

The doc looked horrified.

"No. I'm only kidding! Why do you guys take everything so seriously? I mean, sometimes you feel like shit, like is this the only thing we've been put on the planet to do?"

"Yes?"

"And sometimes you feel great, like that was a bonk and a half."

"This time?"

"Doc, I tell you, I can't frigging remember! Straight up! No word of a lie!"

"You can't remember?" He made notes. "And love? What about that?"

"Love? What's that got to do with it?" He made a good

fist of singing the words and then he laughed nervously again whilst the doctor looked on indulgently. "Come on doc, can you give me Zoya's address? I've got to see her again."

"Why?"

"Because …" He hesitated again and then plunged on. "Because I think it was her."

The doctor showed no surprise. "How old are you Georgi?"

That name again. Maybe it was because they were Russians. Oh no, he'd better not say that or Tomas'd be on his high horse again. They don't like the Russians, he reminded himself. "Thirty three," he lied, "hard paper round. Ha!" And then he thought that was stupid, they had his passport and they could tell at a glance. He covered it over by being brash. "Come on, doc, where does she live? I've told you why I'm so interested!"

The doctor's face remained deadpan as he studied his notes. George got the uneasy feeling he spoke just as much English as he wanted and now he was shutting George out. "Don't you think it's time for you to start rethinking this? That it's not all there is to life?" the doctor asked him.

He seemed to have made a decision. Standing up, he walked to the door. Tomas was standing outside.

George had a notion he'd been listening. So what? He might learn something. "You can come back in now," he said to Tomas.

George thought he looked sheepish as he came in. Hell, he wasn't about to apologise to these bloody commies for the way he was. He lived in the real world. This bunch had a harsh reality awaiting them. He'd almost asked the doctor how much he earned. In a month it was probably what George earned in an hour. "There's no need to hold your meeting here. You can leave," the doctor said and his manner was suddenly brusque, "if you have somewhere to go."

"I've got the hotel to go to," George replied, surprised but pleased.

"No," the doctor said, "I'm only signing you out if you have somewhere to stay where they'll look after you."

"You can come back to my flat," Tomas said, "my wife won't mind."

George shrugged. "If the night doctor's not on duty this week," he said, "not much point in hanging around. I'd still like her address, some means of contacting her."

For the first time the Scouser addressed the question. "Zoya works very hard," he said, "split shits can take it out of you. She's earned her rest. If she wants to contact you, she will. I'll make sure she knows where you are."

He smiled at George and opened the door to leave. "*Labai malonu*, Georgi." Then he was gone.

"I had the distinct impression he was brushing me off," George said, a trifle miffed.

"Oh no, George, I can assure you our doctors are extremely well trained, there is no way, no way I tell you, they would not do a thorough job. They are some of the best doctors in Europe."

George groaned and lay back on his pillow. "Oh, leave it out Tomas," he replied wearily.

CHAPTER 7

Tomas insisted on his company taking care of the bill and George was released into his custody. He was still feeling not quite himself but his new custodian insisted they take a detour by the company so the members of the board would know George's problem was genuine. "Some of the board members are suspicious," he explained. "It is a very large sum of money we are parting with. When you weren't on time for the first meeting they feared the worst."

"But they seemed all right!" George pretended to be mystified but he was concerned deep down in case his little scheme had been rumbled.

"Yes. Well, it was partly put right when you turned up, even though it was late, but, you know how it is, once a bad impression has been created, well, it takes some dispelling."

"But you know what happened!" George said indignantly.

"Of course I do, "Tomas replied soothingly, "but I am not them. I am the new kid on the block. They are worried in case I am part of a scam."

"Scam!" George's voice broke at the top of its register. He was making a real effort to sound suitably indignant.

Tomas's suddenly deeper voice was soothing. "You know it's understandable George! These guys don't know you like I do. Of course they worry about whether we pay big money out and we get nothing back. This is a poor country. We can't afford to part with nearly half a million bucks without some assurances."

"Excuse me, excuse me," George replied, rattled, "you are getting ten million sterling out of this and what is the deposit, five hundred big ones, that's what it is!"

"But you have to understand George that five hundred big ones, five hundred thousand of your Great British pounds, is a king's ransom here in Lithuania." Tomas was wagging his finger as he strode along. George had trouble keeping pace with him, even if he walked with an exaggerated loose and relaxed sway.

"I appreciate that, I appreciate it, kid, but from tiny acorns do great oaks grow, and if yous lads can prove yous have the staying power then yous can be sure the money will be there to back yous. The ten mill is just the starter for ten." George could have kicked himself. He knew exactly why he'd reverted to his northern home dialect: because he was panicky; the incident at the hotel had unnerved him; and he was trying too hard to sound genuine, the man of the people. He cut it out and grinned ingratiatingly. He didn't want a wheel coming off this donkey cart now, not after all he'd been through. The problem was the cart felt a bit like a tumbril. Where had that come from?

"I hope so, George, I hope so," Tomas replied, "but you can understand that people who have to lay these kind of monies out are going to question who is the custodian, it's only natural, isn't it?"

"The problem is there's no trust any more," George moaned. "That's what's wrong with business nowadays. I'm English. My word is my bond."

"Oh, I appreciate that George but we are a bit stupid here, you know. We should take things like that for granted. Instead we check people out."

"What does that mean?"

"We know your investment bank is a very big dealer but it also turns down more business than it writes. My partners merely want to be reassured that they will not become another statistic of rejected business after paying out such a large deposit. You can understand that, can't you?"

The irony was a little above George's head but even so he was nonplussed that Tomas had done his homework. The indictment of his bank's approach to investment business was spot on. George was nothing if not streetwise, though; there was no point in going against the flow; this needed a change of tack: congratulate them for their caution and nous; deal with it. Once set on that course he breezed through it. "Stands to reason, kid, let's get this shit out of the way, eh? Wheel me in. I'll satisfy them. As long as you stick to the letter of the deal, no problemo. Now what do you think about that?

"No, what do you think about *that*?" Tomas replied.

They had stopped by a statue. "What?" George asked, puzzled by the question. Here he was thinking business and Tomas had stopped in front of a lump of old stone.

"That is the Grand Duke Gediminas."

"Who's he when he's at home?"

"The Grand Duke is a great Lithuanian hero. " Tomas's chest puffed out proudly. "Do you know that once he controlled the largest state in Europe from the Lithuanian forests over to the Ukraine as far as Kiev?"

"Oh, you're having me on!"

"My wife, Aldona, comes from Kiev. We were pagans then."

The curious juxtaposition of sentences had George baffled for a moment. "What, you? I've never been much of a one for religion myself but I wouldn't describe myself as pagan neither."

"No, I am sure you are taking advantage of my lack of English now, George. I didn't mean we are pagans now, of course not. Aldona and I are Roman Catholics. I meant we, the Lithuanian people, were the last pagan state in Europe."

George was utterly bewildered now as to why that should concern him. Casting one more glance up at the forbidding visage of the ancient Grand Duke, he scuttled off in pursuit of Tomas's clicking heels. Further on they walked through a square. In the middle was a stone plinth. On it stood the remnants of another statue, but it was just a foot and leg truncated below the knee. George stopped and looked at it, puzzled. "What the fuck is that?" he asked.

"From the sublime to the ridiculous," Tomas laughed. "That's our little joke. It was a statue of Lenin. I was there when the crane ripped it out of the ground. We've left that bit to remind us that, not so long ago, we were an occupied nation but that this, in the end, is what becomes of all tyrants."

"What happened to the rest of it?" George asked.

"We put the rest of him in a public park. A kind of show trial! Neat, eh? "

George shook his head. He knew he was a bit slow after

his recent experiences but was Tomas taking the piss now? If so, what was the board meeting going to be like? He was right to be worried. The meeting turned out to be a very Eastern European affair. Dark glowerings from the other side of the table accompanied George's attempts, in his weakened state, to convince them this deal was no con. What had happened to them he wondered? They were all right before. Towards the end he seemed to be winning them over but the effort had left him exhausted. "If I thought I was coming out here for a good time, kid," he told Tomas, while mopping his brow during a comfort break, "I had another think coming. I feel like I've been through the pork mincer a dozen times."

"And you haven't even met the man yet," Tomas replied gloomily.

George started as if he'd suffered an electric shock. "The man? Who the hell is the man?" No one had warned him to expect a hidden player. So that's why they were suddenly so disapproving.

"The man who owns the majority of the shares," Tomas said, "nothing happens unless he says so."

George breathed in deeply. "What, you mean there's a frigging man from Del Monte and I'm dealing with the frigging tomatoes?"

"I'm sorry, I don't understand," Tomas replied.

George shrugged wearily, temporarily defeated. "You'll have to take me back to your place, kid, because I'm finding this tough going. I mean do these guys want to do a deal or don't they? I can just as easily get the next plane out of here." He wondered how he'd explain that to Marty when up to now he'd said they'd been eating out of his hand but you had to bluff didn't you?

Tomas nodded sympathetically. He went out and told everyone George was tired. Suddenly they were sympathetic too. They came back in and while he sat there they began to clap him. He could have been sitting at the Communist Party Congress. All these guys in grey suits applauding him! When he'd got over waving his acknowledgments, he felt like a coffin in a funeral procession. "Okay," the one called Audrius, who had been among the most searching in his enquiries, said at length. He held up his hand so that the applause stopped immediately, just as it had started, without spontaneity, as if it was something they always did. "Just wait a short time," he added to George, "sign the minute of the meeting and then we'll adjourn."

The minutes were passed across. Tomas signed them and gave them to George to sign. He squinted at them. They were written in Lithuanian. "I can't understand this," he said.

"It's no problem George," Tomas said, "here, this is what we discussed, " and, pointing at the print with his biro as if that would somehow translate it, he outlined the minutes of the meeting to George, who, somewhat reluctantly, at last put pen to paper. "That's a good thing, George," Tomas said, "there were a few doubters here today and the trust you have shown in us will go down well. It is already making some of my comrades ashamed."

"Comrades?" George asked, disconcerted by the choice of noun.

Tomas banged his forehead. "Did I say that? Old habits do die hard, George. I meant colleagues of course."

"Right," George said, "let's remember that, shall we, and, by the way, can we get out of here now?"

"Of course, of course," Tomas replied soothingly. But maddeningly Tomas was one of those people who never actually got anywhere. There was always something else for him to do. George made a mental note that he didn't concentrate properly. He was forever flitting on to the next thing. He always had two mobile phones on the go, which he talked on at great length in his gibberish of a language, even when he was in the middle of talking to someone else about something totally different. He decided there and then that, if he ever got in that confrontational situation with Tomas where he had to tell him straight why he'd done what he'd done, he'd just use that. Observed you over time, kid, and decided you just couldn't cut it so I cut you instead.

Visibly seething he was quite looking forward to that
day of reckoning when, eventually, Tomas found a gap
in his busy schedule and said brightly, "come on then
George, don't hang around, I must take you back to
meet Aldona, my wife." About time too George was
muttering to himself as he dragged his heavy limbs off
the chair but even then Tomas added: "Unfortunately,
we must make another short detour on the way."
George groaned audibly and Tomas continued quickly:
"yes, business is business as I am sure you appreciate
more than most, a hard-working man like you. It seems
there has been an accident at one of the factories so I
have to go home via the Panevezys road."

"Panevezys!" George exploded. Even with his limited
knowledge of the landscape he had an idea of distances.
"That must be at least a hundred kliks!" he spluttered.

Tomas laughed. "Never mind, it's not all the way to
Panevezys. We'll be there and back in no time, and in
the meantime I can tell you how the Grand Duke and
my ancestors defeated the Teutonic Knights."

"This trip will pass in a jiffy!"

"A jiffy?"

George groaned. "Never mind."

They reached the factory an hour later. It might not have been all the way to Panevezys but it was ninety per cent and it was stuck in the middle of the deepest, darkest forest George had ever seen. Mist drifted up from the frozen ground as he climbed out of the car. He looked round suspiciously as if he expected to see the wraiths of ancient knights emerging through the mist. He shivered. Tomas's tales, with which he had been regaled in the car, of the battles between the Grand Duchy and the Teutonic Knights in these very forests had sparked even his imagination. The factory was in fact a massive timber mill. George followed Tomas in. Huge saws whirred and whined as they stripped the bark off trees and sliced through oak logs. Workmen ran around in droves and George was horrified to see some did not even have shoes. The machinery was largely unguarded. It was a health and safety nightmare. Tomas seemed to read his thoughts because he said apologetically, "we are trying but change is slow. This is why you get such a good deal for your money, George. This is why labour is cheaper here. There aren't so many regulations."

"You're right, kid," George replied, "they've got it too soft back home. Frigging unions, they've ruined the country!" Unable to understand a word of Tomas's interminable conversations with supervisors and charge hands he decided to leave his host to his own devices and wandered outside. More workers slaved out there in the freezing night, stacking the woodpiles and loading the trailers.

It was a pretty big enterprise. Tomas seemed to have good connections. An enterprising capitalist who took the long view, or even a mid-term perspective, could make a fortune here. Unfortunately George was still an adherent of Marty Freeman's economic philosophy and tended to believe you were either quick or dead. In and out, just like that – almost unconsciously he made a swift movement with his arm. It was like a cobra striking. On your toes all the time. It's kind of like bank robbery: you arrive, take out the guards; the countdown begins and then you're out of there, millions richer, but you left behind what timed out. It was a good, disciplined philosophy. Why risk everything on long term bets which might or might not come off?

Lost in his thoughts but suffering from a guilty conscience because he really believed these guys could buck the trend, George had meandered closer to the forest. It was like a wall. Through the mist, which hung in ghostly fashion between the trees, he caught sight of phantoms. Was that a fire burning over there? He ventured into the trees and saw ghostly figures standing round a bonfire. There was a spit over it and on it hung a creature. Was it a wild boar? He had a flashback to his weird dream of …. when? How long had he been here? It seemed an age. Scared and curious at the same time he stumbled over the rough ground towards the scene where workers in their rough animal furs piled wood on the fire. They moved around as if regimented - slow like automatons but with a purpose to every movement. The closer he got, the more he wondered, just as he had in the dream, if the creature on the spit was a man. Then he heard a voice calling and Tomas emerged out of the mist. "There you are, George! I was worried about you for a moment. You should not wander off by yourself into the forest. You could very easily become lost and then who knows if we would ever find you? There are very deep marshes out there and they have their secrets. Many a foreigner has been drowned in them."

"Why only foreigners?" George asked, puzzled by Tomas's precision.

"Our Lithuanian forests do not swallow our own people," Tomas assured him. "The nationals they keep safe. They devour only the foreign hordes who ride against our people." He smiled at George in a way which, for all the illogicality, brooked no argument, as if his words were imbued with a kind of papal infallibility. Weird, George was thinking. Tomas could come across as the most rational person imaginable and then he'd blurt out crap like that! He was glad to climb back into the car, particularly when the rudimentary heater started blowing hot air.

On the way back, through a darkness as dense as stone, he became lost in his own thoughts. His estranged wife figured deeply in them. Someone had hinted to him that she was on the verge of starting another relationship with a younger man. He seethed with resentment at the thought of supporting a toy boy. It didn't occur to him that the man might be self-supporting, that he might want to be with his wife, the older woman, because of who she was, not the meal ticket she provided vicariously. Meanwhile, Tomas had fallen into a brooding silence as if he knew that George's mood was not one to be disturbed. The depth of the darkness and the black ice on the roads hindered progress to the extent that it was another one and half hours before they limped back into Vilnius and headed towards Tomas's apartment block. No time he said, George thought, back before they left the city for the forest, no fucking time. And it was as if time did not count here, as if he'd been here years but hadn't noticed them go by. His mind went back to that image on the bonfire.

CHAPTER 8

George had made a number of assumptions about Tomas's wife and all of them were shattered on this first meeting. Appreciating that his young associate had the looks of a rather effete and consumptive male model to go with no small intellect, George still thought him more than merely a touch effeminate. It was only logical, therefore, to expect that his wife would be similarly flawed. On the contrary, Aldona turned out to be of medium height and so voluptuous of figure that she made Mariah Carey look like a stick insect. She also made George feel like he had a steel rod down his pants and he was sure she'd noticed. She was a strawberry blond with a triangular face and very sexy brown eyes, which set up a delicious contrast with her fairness. "Labai malonu!" George greeted her, copying what he'd learned from the Scouser, and he was wondering already what a gorgeous female like this was doing with a nerd like Tomas.

She seemed delighted at this greeting in her own tongue and she put down the sheets and blankets she was carrying in preparation for his stay. She wiped her palms self-consciously then her hand lingered in his, making him feel welcome. Her delight quickly turned to concern for her guest. "Are you all right?" she asked haltingly, striving for familiarity with English. "I know you had bad first day in Lithuania. I hope we make you feel better about us."

George was thinking that one night with her would go a long way but Tomas intervened and said, "He hasn't experienced real Lithuanian hospitality yet, he has to undergo the ritual first." Even though he was addressing Aldona, he said it in English so George would understand.

Aldona put her hand to her mouth in astonishment. "I forgot," she said, "it's bad luck to forget."

"Forgot what? What ritual?" George questioned, his slack jaw drooping and bottom lip stubbornly protruding. There was always a bloody surprise with these Lithuanians. Nothing was normal.

"Oh yes," Tomas said, "you have to......!" and then his voice broke off and he shrugged. Giggling like a schoolgirl, Aldona rushed over to a cupboard near the entrance and opened the door. George couldn't figure out what she was up to but he was enjoying the view of her firm but ample behind, hemispherical in the tight skirt, as she bent over and rummaged in the cupboard. She came back up eventually, the silly grin still on her face, looking at him expectantly as she held out a key on the end of a piece of twine. George did a double-take as it dangled from her long fingers. "While you are staying with us," Tomas began to explain, "you can enter every room. Except one. You must not enter our room." He pointed at a half-closed door through which George could see a double bed and a small en-suite bathroom beyond.

"Why would I want to go into your room?" he asked but he was already thinking of one good reason, but Tomas wouldn't be around then, would he?

The younger man held the key out to George. "This is the key. We keep it in the bureau in the living room. You must not use it. Can we trust you? You must swear not to use it!"

George exploded. He was an international banker for Christ's sake! Didn't they realise how important that made him?

"No, no, you see, George," Tomas continued in his reasonable tones, "it is a ritual in every Lithuanian household. You know, we were a pagan race for a long time, and now whenever a guest comes we show them they can trust us. And in return we ask that we can trust them?"

"Trust them?"

"Yes. That they will not draw swords on us while we sleep? That they will not hurt our kin, or lust after our women." He gave George a meaningful look which suggested he might have guessed what George had been thinking before, which was ridiculous: he was a poker player was George; no one guessed what he was thinking. He looked at Tomas askance, his jaw hitting his boots. Aldona looked at the key again and she gave a kind of wink towards it. George could have sworn it was a leer, the sexy minx! Tomas hadn't noticed his wife's gesture. "You must swear on your children's lives, on what you hold most dear, that you will not use the key!"

"I am not swearing any frigging thing, pal, you can go and get a woolly one up you."

"A woolly one?" Tomas repeated rhetorically. "A woolly one?" he asked Aldona as if seeking inspiration from her. George didn't enlighten him. Then Tomas laughed. "Ah, I see, you think it is some trick!" He turned and said something in Lithuanian to Aldona. She put her hand to her mouth and began to shake uncontrollably.

It wasn't an unpleasant sight with everything jiggling about nicely and there was no doubt that it interfered with George's concentration in a potentially noticeable way. He hid it by pretending to look at his two hosts in his best bewildered fashion. Obviously he'd got the wrong end of the stick. "Will you stop screwing around with my head!" he all but shouted, thinking he could get away with acting the bully. They both looked at him in shock. "All right, I swear on my mother's life, my kids' lives, no, most precious of all, my own life, what the hell! Will that do?"

Aldona's face suggested hurt. Tomas laughed and said, "of course, of course, some customs offend, it is very understandable." He clapped his hands and Aldona's miserable expression disappeared immediately and she became vibrant again. It was like clockwork and she was like a Stepford wife, reacting to her husband's mood. Maybe he was a bit more of an alpha male than George had given him credit for. Tomas changed the subject and suggested George might like some soup or maybe even something more substantial.

A little yellowy brown dog peeped round the door. George didn't like dogs. This one growled at him softly. "There, there," Aldona said, rushing to calm it down. She picked it up and fondled it like a baby. "Look we have a visitor," she said. George found himself having to force a smile but made up his mind to kick the mutt as soon as no one was looking.

"It can't talk, can it?" he asked doubtfully. You never knew with these bloody people!

"Don't be silly, of course he can!" Aldona put the little dog down and shooed it back in the living room.

George now regretted his momentary outburst. He still wasn't himself. He tried to join in with the spirit of the thing. Language and customs are funny things. He didn't know precisely what Tomas had been getting at but least said soonest mended. "So it's get your pinny on pet," he said affably to Aldona, realising his stance had embarrassed his hosts and trying to make up for it. Aldona didn't appear to understand. Her English was okay when she was speaking but not very good when she was hearing it. George figured this out when Tomas went to the loo and he followed Aldona into the kitchen. He was trying to soft soap her. "You've got a nice little place here," he said.

"Oh yes," she replied, "I love cook."

"No, no, I mean it's really nice this kitchen."

"Oh yeah, it's silent area."

"Silent area?" It took him a moment to appreciate she meant the neighbourhood.

She saw the problem. "Oh, Tomas he the one who talk English. Really well."

"Yeah? He's such a clever so and so, isn't he? And you don't?" George asked.

"Oh, no, no," she replied.

"What would you say if I told you you've got a gorgeous figure?"

"Oh, smashing."

"And I'd like to get better acquainted with it?"

"Yeah, yeah, great."

"Make sexy rhythms," and he swivelled his hips in time to an imaginary music.

"Hey, disco, you mean, you like dance?" The bewilderment left her face. She was on the same wavelength now.

"Yeah, I like the horizontal dance best, baby." He was already feeling much better when her husband returned from the bathroom. Even so Tomas seemed to have picked up something of the vibe because he stared at them suspiciously. George shrugged. Tough, that's what it was. He couldn't help being a super-attractive specimen of the male of the species. Pity about the bald patch, though. And the eyesight! Jeez! He was falling apart.

Later, after Aldona had gone to bed, Tomas confided in him that things hadn't gone terribly well since they'd got married. It had made him sort of....sort of... He had difficulty not with the concept, George guessed, but with coming out with it, so George helped him in his inimitably subtle way: "impotent?" he queried.

"Yeah, no, kind of," Tomas said looking crestfallen.

"Can't get it up, eh?"

"Okay, okay." It was obvious the younger man regretted opening up.

"Well you should lighten up. If I was you I'd go up there and give your good lady one right now." Tomas looked uncomfortable. "But I'm not you," George added, "so you'll probably sit here and talk to me and drink whisky and wonder why things aren't going right between you."

"But you know how it is George, you are divorcing. Things didn't work out for you."

Funny, George thought. He didn't remember telling Tomas that. He wasn't that loose-tongued about his personal relationships. He worked on the need to know basis. He'd told the doctor because it might have been important to the cure, but he couldn't conceive of the doctor repeating it to Tomas, it would be a breach of that hypocritic oath or whatever. Then he remembered: the bugger must have been listening at the door! "Hey, hold your horses, sunshine, "George said, "me and our Jen were together for fifteen years before that happened, and I didn't want it to happen, mind. Believe me, it wasn't for lack of that either! So yous've got a long way to go yet, and if I was you I'd start tonight. Before someone else starts for yous."

Tomas still looked uncomfortable. "You see, George," he said, "it is easy for you but here it is all business. We are too busy earning a living to enjoy life. Not like you. You have it all nicely compartmentalised."

George thought about this for a moment. "Priorities, kid," he said at length. "Don't let the important things in life pass you by."

"Is that what you've done George?"

The question was innocent but even so it was crushing. George looked back into Tomas's clear blue eyes for a moment and he could think of a retort or two but he decided not to bother. There was another way to prove his point and the plan was already formulating in his mind. "So how do you think the meeting went?" he asked, adroitly changing the subject, knowing Tomas would not miss a moment's conversation about business. He ought to get a life, but he wouldn't.

"Well," Tomas replied, "I think it went well. Audrius was very impressed with you and he has some sway. You see, George it has been very hard for them to overcome this idea that everything is a rip off."

"You've not dealt with us, that's why kid."

"Well, even so, George, as I explained, we did some due diligence on your company."

Did Tomas see George flinch? He hoped not. He'd thought this particular nettle had already been grasped, he didn't want to return to it time and time again. "Oh, yeah," he said, "and I thought we'd dealt with that, but no doubt you're going to tell me how it panned out?"

"So, so," Tomas replied totally deadpan, ignoring the sarcasm, "we found out you only do one of about a hundred deals you look at."

"Hey, it's not that low a percentage," George replied, but he was already on the back foot and even what he'd just said was a bigger admission than he'd have wanted to make. Tomas was very skilful the way he'd drawn that out. He'd have to watch him. He was cleverer than he'd given him credit for. What was it about these Eastern Europeans? They were all good at chess, weren't they? He blustered on, trying to cover up his gaffe, "but that's the way it is kid, if they don't stack up, you've got to jettison them."

"Yes," Tomas said, "but the trick is you earn commission from every one you look at."

George flinched again. It probably wasn't visible to the outside world. It was the merest swallow, a flicker of the eyelids, a twitch of the jaw. Tomas showed no sign of having noticed. "I believe in doing nothing if you don't get paid," George said. "No point in looking into any deal if you've got to use your own money just to check it out."

"No, no, I commend you," Tomas replied, "very good

business if you can get it, but you can see how it would make my board nervous. At least I thought that before today's meeting."

George pricked up his ears. "So what happened at today's meeting then?" he asked, hoping he didn't sound as anxious as he felt.

"Audrius said you're just the kind of guy we need," Tomas replied, "someone to harden up the edges. We are too damn naive. We have been in the Soviet system too long and it was wasteful. We need someone who looks for profit in every deal, in every detail of every deal. They have confidence in you, George, they have confidence in their project and they have confidence in you to swing your people behind it. They are thinking of asking you to be the bank's board nominee, so we can get the benefit of your knowledge." He paused then added as if he had forgotten, "for a fee of course. We would not dream of not paying you for your valuable services."

George heaved an indiscernible sigh of relief and winked at him. "He's a shrewd operator, that Audrius," he replied. "I think he'll go far. He's learned the secret of business, it's not about helping people, it's about profit, money. Money, I love it." He gave the appearance of thinking about it before he added: "yeah, although I don't usually do the nominee thing, we leave that to the accountants, I might on this occasion, I can see the benefits of going with you guys precisely because there's people like you there and people like Audrius. This is one hell of a country for development opportunities. The potential's enormous. Mega. The sky's the limit!"

He thought, if that's what it takes to swing the deal, no problemo, I'll pretend to go along with it. In fact he only realised himself that he was bullshitting when he saw that Tomas was regarding him with what seemed almost like concentrated pity - if he hadn't known better! Why should a poor, untutored sod like Tomas, who had just confessed that he couldn't even get it up his newlywed wife, look at him with sympathy in his eyes? Tomas replied gently, his voice carrying to George a hint of sarcasm. "Someone told us you were the investment bank that wrote all the business you can and then you carry out the promises you see fit. If anyone sues, you fight, if it gets tough you settle, but you always make a profit."

"Sounds to me like yous've been talking to one of the competition," George said. "Jealous bastards, all of them."

Tomas burst into uncontrolled laughter and when it subsided he poured George another whisky. Aldona put her head round the door to say goodnight. She had her nightie on and George looked approvingly at her figure. The gown wasn't see through but it was sort of translucent, you got more than just the shape and she certainly wasn't wearing knickers underneath it. He

118

didn't hide his interest either, such was his ingrained narcissism. Aldona in turn looked disapprovingly at George's whisky and started to talk to Tomas. George could tell from the body language and the pitch that she was berating him for giving him hard spirits in his medical condition. He tried to acclimatise to the sounds. He'd never been much of a one for languages but he'd lived in a lot of places in his time so he picked up similarities of sounds. His heart chilled suddenly. As Aldona spoke he heard her say the name "Zoya." Then Tomas repeated it, he seemed to be arguing back. Trying not to give anything away George concentrated hard but his senses were swimming. He found himself concentrating on the exchange and then Zoya's name was mentioned again.

After saying goodnight to the scolding Aldona and thanking her for her concern about his welfare George said quietly to Tomas, "I heard you mention Zoya when you were talking."

Tomas immediately looked edgy. "What...what...?" He seemed all of a sudden to be at sixes and sevens with his English and this time George was in the ascendant but he didn't let him off the hook. He persisted and Tomas replied, "Yes, yes, Aldona was talking about her sister-in-law."

"Aldona's sister-in-law is called Zoya?" George asked nonplussed.

"Yes," Tomas replied defensively, "it's a common enough name. You're not still talking about that woman are you?"

"The night doctor!" George exclaimed.

"George, you're hallucinating, the night doctor might have the familiar name Zoya but she's not the woman you met in the bar. Whatever happened to you, it put you into delirium and you are confusing the two."

"How do you know?" George asked. "Maybe I'm not."

"Don't be stupid, George, if she was working the night shift at the hospital how could she be in the bar? You heard the doctor tell us she'd just finished the night shift last night so she must have been working the whole week!" He looked at George almost scornfully as if he had defeated him by superior logic.

George was still troubled by it shortly after in the cramped spare room. Was every woman in the Baltics called Zoya? Was it a bit like the Arabs where everyone was called Ben, the Scots Mac or the Irish Fitz? And why should Aldona mention it when she was scolding Tomas for giving George whisky? It had sounded as if she was saying Zoya wouldn't approve. Why should Zoya not approve unless she was a doctor? Actually then he realised the extent to which he was speculating and it even sounded ridiculous to him. You must be away with the mixer if you're starting to believe that,

Giorgio, he told himself. Still, it was about then the slight wounds on his wrist began to itch, as if reminding him there was something else he'd forgotten. It was like cat scratches, the way they smart for ages afterwards. He put the light out and lay down on the bed. Soon he was in a shallow, troubled sleep. Zoya was standing there again, but she wasn't wearing her doctor's smock. No, she was wearing a flimsy number and she was starting to take it off. In his dream he awoke just as she slipped out of the door again. He was too tired to get up and check the corridor. Had he dreamt about her again? This was an awful predicament. He couldn't tell when he was awake or dreaming.

CHAPTER 9

Next morning he woke up feeling more like his old self if not exactly full of the joys of spring. His introduction to Lithuania had been a bit of an unusual baptism but he was philosophical. Nothing much had been lost, and there were prospects. As if to bear out this change of mood Tomas dropped in on him just before going to work. "Remember I need that Letter of Credit," George told him.

"No problem, not after yesterday's meeting, I feel," Tomas replied cheerfully, "it should be available today. Maybe tomorrow if the man decides he wants to check a couple of details."

The man, the man, there it was again. "Who is this bloody man? Is it Audrius? I thought you said he was okay with it?"

"No, no, not Audrius. He is the chief accountant, the sort of FD, not the CEO. He wasn't there yesterday, the main man."

George groaned but he wasn't going to let it throw him; he was getting back to his swaggering best. "What is there left to check? I thought I did all that in the meeting! What was the point of yesterday if it wasn't the full Monty? Now don't let your people think they can screw with me Tomas, I can get straight on the plane and go after a dozen deals bigger than this one. I'm doing this because I like yous and your people. But you can go off folk. Be warned! They want to get their heads in gear those guys, and put pen to paper, get the readies across." George flicked the thumb and first two fingers of his right hand together - once again the international sign of the deal.

"Oh yes, George, I think everything was quite satisfactory.... but it is a large sum of money."

"You worry me! Every time I get this thing of ours sorted out with you, you come back to the same petty point! It's getting like a vicious circle. Yous keep saying that kid and I keep saying it's not, it's seed capital only. Think what yous're getting back! Get real!" George pointed a finger at him, then at his own head, "you guys must be crazy if you cock on this deal, no skin off my nose, am I bothered?" He shrugged.

"What we are getting back? In three months yes," Tomas replied patiently as if lecturing an errant schoolchild for the umpteenth time on some aberration of behaviour the child was unable to address, "that's when we get something back, and yes, okay, it is big bucks, it is the chance to really go ahead and finish something here in this country, but it is the wait in between, George, that is the trouble, the biting of the fingernails while your bank does its due diligence, worrying in case anything crawls out of the woodwork and then we end up further back than the Soviets!"

George shrugged again, his bottom lip folding over downwards as if it was nothing to him. "Those are the rules, kid, that's the wave we came in on, that's the way we do things. If you want to play with the big boys you play by the big boys' rules." He looked at Tomas archly and added in his cocky manner, "why, is something going to crawl out the woodwork?" That was the best technique, always put the ball back in their court. You always knew the answer. They had to say no way, and then you could say, so what's the problem then?

It worked like a charm. Tomas couldn't answer it directly so he contented himself with, "anyway, leave it with me, I'll do my best to finalise it today. Tomorrow you should be able to ring home and find the money … what did you say? Plummeting out of the sky?"

"It'd better be," George warned, consciously keeping the pressure on the younger man, who, he was finding, always crumbled under this kind of pressure, "or I might just pull the rug on this whole deal. It's not been such a brilliant trip so far." It was unfair but he knew it would hit a nerve with Tomas's patriotism.

"No, no, I'm sorry about that," Tomas replied, crestfallen, "I really feel ashamed of my country."

"Okay, kid, it wasn't your fault," George said, knowing

this battle was won, Tomas was going in to push the LC through like yesterday. That's how you did it, make someone else take the responsibility. Business was always about the jungle. Always about making the baboons do the work and trap the prey and then you amble up at your leisure and take the kill off them while they stand screeching at you from a safe distance. He breathed on his fingernails. "I think I'll ring home today," he added, "but my mobile's run down. Can I charge it?"

"I doubt we have an adaptor. Do you have one?"

George sighed. What kind of one horse town was this? "Okay, can I use your land line?"

Tomas reverted to his cheerful self. He just loved to do you a favour. He wanted to be liked. That was a great weakness. "Of course, help yourself, remember we're an hour ahead. I have to go now but Aldona will make you some breakfast before she goes to work."

"Hey, that's great, okay, kid, see you," he said. "Ciao!" He waved his right hand in an arrogant salutation, a man totally in command. Tomas smiled back and left the older man to rest. George, feeling a little light-headed after all that effort, lay back on the pillow. A few minutes later there was a knock on the door. "Come in," he said. It was Aldona and she'd brought him a cup of coffee. "Thanks sweetheart," he said. She was wearing a bathrobe and he stared at her boldly because, tied tightly across the waist, it showed off what he already knew - she had a great figure. He felt the stirrings of unsatisfied passion as he remembered his feelings from the night before. Oh, yes and there was the mystery of her sister. Instinctively, he groaned and closed his eyes, lying back even deeper into his pillow.

Aldona immediately looked concerned. "Are you okay?" she asked him, her English still a little halting and lacking in confidence.

"Yeah, yeah," he replied, pushing himself up on one elbow and shaking his head groggily, "I just get bouts, that's all." Despite the appearance he was trying to give, he felt like patting her backside as she put the cup down but realised that might be a step too far.

Without realising it, however, Aldona gave him the perfect lead in. "Tomas is really nervous you do this deal," she said.

"Oh yeah?" he pricked up his ears. "Well I might. Can't guarantee it, mind!" He wagged a finger as he took a sip of the coffee. Wonder of wonders, Aldona was sprucing up the pillows behind his back. He could smell her perfume, it made him feel heady, and the cleavage as her robe fell partly open in the inclining movement gave promise of spectacular bliss. "It mean so much to him," Aldona went on as she worked expertly, making him wonder if she was a nurse, "he really need this break, he is able to run that factory. I wish there is something I do to persuade you."

"Maybe there is," George said. It was now or never, faint heart never won fair lady, and forget about loyalty to your colleagues and all that nonsense, the love game isn't a team thing, so he reached out and goosed her shapely bottom. She looked momentarily taken aback and he thought for a moment he'd mistimed it, ruined it for good, maybe done a bit of damage, then, wonder of wonders, she just slipped out of the bathrobe and she was totally naked. He caught his breath. Her hair fell loosely over milk white breasts, hiding them, inviting his hands to part those tresses and take the plump prizes. He made no move to conceal the bulge in the middle of the duvet. Aldona leant over him as he squeezed her breasts. She looked at the bulge, the ghost of a smile on her lips. His eyes indicated what he wanted. Laughing, she pulled the duvet back and fell on his member, first sucking and then laving each side and the tip. George had both tits in his hands as if weighing them. "Two kilos of best Baltic," he quipped, "you don't get many of those to the pound!" Casually, as if it meant nothing more than an exercise, she bestrode him, mouth half open as she lowered herself. She breathed out audibly as it slid in to the hilt. He massaged her, making her mouth and eyes open in spectacular O's.

But to her it seemed all in a day's work. She pulled off him wetly, picked up the robe and sauntered off to the bathroom. At the door she waved in her nakedness, but she showed she had her wits about her and that something other than a passion for his body had been the impulse for their coupling when she threw in, "make sure you do that deal!"

"No problemo, sweetheart," he said, "hope that was okay for you?" She patted her comely ass in response and he took that as a gesture of satisfaction. "Plenty more where that came from!" he called. She smirked and shut the door behind her. Wonder if she always leaves after Tomas, he thought, and he wasn't the slightest bit bothered if she was only doing it to ensure he did his best for Tomas. He'd row in with that as far as necessary, making all the right noises without actually making any firm commitment...

A little later he heard her singing in the bath. That's the effect he had. He put on his jeans and went out of the room. The little yellow dog lay on the carpet in the hall, looking up at him. There was something accusatory in that look. "Who the hell do you think you're looking at?" he said, and he toe-poked it, laughing as the small beast slunk away. "I'm shafting you because I can," he told himself in the hall mirror, but he wasn't really talking to himself, he was talking to Tomas, psyching himself up. There was something jumped up about the lad, too clever for his own good, and too pretty-pretty. He suffered from the delusion that he was premier league. It was good he'd banged his wife, and, judging by the way she'd lapped it up, he wasn't the only one who thought that way. She'd needed a good seeing to.

Then suddenly he became nervous. The flat might be bugged! It wasn't so long since the secret police days. But he thought of the romp on the bed. No way would Aldona have done that if the flat was bugged. Unless, of course, Tomas was bugging her too. "He bloody well should," he exclaimed. There was the poor idiot drowning in his work and worrying about the effect it was having on his marriage, confiding in George of all people about his fear of impotence, George, who sympathised with him on the surface just to see how he could use it to his own advantage! But hadn't he done everyone a favour? She was going to be happier; Tomas would pick up on that. In no time at all they'd be at it again. Oh, just a minute, would that make him redundant?

He was in the middle of this self-justification when Aldona appeared, dressed for work. She looked perplexed, straight through him, as if he were invisible. "Have you seen where my bag?" she asked as if he should know. He was feeling horny again and let her know but she was distant, letting him nuzzle her affectionately but she seemed oblivious to the hard evidence of his reawakening and she turned her lips away so he could kiss only her cheek. He remembered she had done that when they made love. Everything else, many things which an impartial observer would see as more intimate, but not a kiss on the mouth. It became a momentary obsession to get her to kiss him but he got nowhere. She was cold and seemed to be concentrating on checking her phone. Giving up, it suddenly occurred to him to ask her something. "Who's Zoya?"

She wasn't remotely evasive - as everyone else had been when the mystery woman was named. "Tomas's sister," she replied.

"Tomas's sister?" He was rocked back on his heels, Tomas had said she was Aldona's sister-in-law. Oh I get it, he thought. Then he didn't. Why would he say that? Why would he not say she was his sister? And then he remembered the look of the girl in the bar and his thought that her bone structure had reminded him vaguely of someone. Of course, it was Tomas.

"She's a beauty. Not like me."

He was soft-soaping now, in need of information. "You underestimate yourself," he replied with an attempt at gallantry.

"Zoya doesn't have ginger hair and freckles," she laughed. "And she's tall and slim."

His pulse quickened. "I call you strawberry blond," he lied, "but what is she, dark or fair?"

"Dark, very dark," she replied, "she has the Ukrainian side of Tomas's family in her. She was born with the beauty and brains."

"Brains? What does she do?"

"She's a doctor, at the hospital here. I thought you knew that. I thought you'd met her."

"A doctor?"

"Yeah. And she specialises in transcendentalism."

His head was reeling now. He was so shocked it didn't even occur to him to ask what transcendentalism was. Tomas had lied to him brazenly but he was so inept that here was his wife just coming out with it matter-of-factly as if there was nothing to hide. "I think I did meet her," he said. There were warning bells going off in his head. Worse than that, a whole screaming aviary was banging against the internal walls of his skull. Jesus, this is trouble, he was thinking. I have got to get out of here.

"Anyway, I've got to go to work," Aldona prattled on, "I'm late already. "You'll meet Zoya again. She'll be round to see us tonight. I know she'll want to see how you are."

George didn't know whether to be pleased or shit-scared. He rose quickly to disguise his discomfort and continued the gallantry line: "And I'll look forward to meeting her again," he said, "in different circumstances I hope." Aldona nodded vaguely but she didn't appear to know what he meant. She would think he was talking about the hospital, and partly he was, but did she know about the nightclub? Maybe she did know about the nightclub and the hotel, maybe they'd all had a good laugh about it, the stupid Englishman, such a dodo he let someone knock him senseless and tie him up in the bath. Then another thing occurred to him, was it his imagination or had Aldona's English suddenly improved? Last night she couldn't string two words together; today she'd been gabbling away like it was a second language. Was that the effect of a close encounter with him? If so, he should bottle it and make a fortune. George's language school. A quick injection and you'll speak English like a native!

CHAPTER 10

Aldona at last found her handbag and went to work. George heard the lock click. He was trying to keep his emotions under control. There had to be a rational explanation for all this. He decided to report back into the office and see what the score was, maybe it would even be worth asking Marty what he made of it. When he thought about it, though, he realised that might be putting his head in the lion's mouth. He could just be waiting for an opportunity to bite it off.

He picked up the phone and began dialling but nothing happened. He tried again then he realised the phone was dead. "What a bloody country!" he cursed. He'd have to find a public phone. Grabbing his coat he tried the front door but it wouldn't open. "Oh no, don't say she locked it!" he shouted. He couldn't see a key. It would be under a bowl or hanging near the door or on the hall stand. He searched. There was nothing. He went through to the back door and found it locked too on the same sort of super-strength deadlock system. Why did they need that kind of security? And then of course he remembered it was because there were some poor people here, some lawless, poor people. Everyone was security conscious. He went to a window and looked out. The apartment was on the tenth floor. He was a prisoner. "What the hell's going on?" he screamed at no one in particular. Heading for the front door he hammered on it, thinking if the neighbours heard him they might know to ring Tomas or Aldona at work. There was no response. He banged away for a quarter of an hour or so, perhaps longer, but it was getting him nowhere.

Eventually he gave up, exhausted. He sat down on the settee in the front room and tried to collect his thoughts. The stupid little brown dog was looking at him. Why did people keep dogs cooped up in flats, he wondered? "Bugger off!" he shouted and in his frustration he kicked the dog. It yelped and rushed off under the table. Feeling ill at ease, he went into the kitchen and made himself a cup of tea. Normally he didn't take sugar but today he tried two to get his glucose levels up. He found the toaster and toasted himself a couple of slices of bread, buttering it heavily. He began to feel more like his old self. There had to be a rational explanation for all this. Maybe Aldona had just made a mistake. She gave the impression of being a bit scatty at the best of times. Perhaps his gift of a morning shot had affected her, a kind of delayed reaction. She had seemed distant afterwards. Maybe it had really got on her mind. The best way to handle it was to turn it to his advantage. He'd think about how. Then he fell asleep. His antics of the last few days had worn him out too.

When he awoke it was well past midday. He walked around the apartment, studying it carefully. There was nothing which could really be said to bear the stamp of its owners. It was all fairly anonymous. The pictures on the wall of country scenes were the same as you might find anywhere. There was something going insistently through his head. The slant of the light in the afternoon gave the place a gloomy appearance not unlike that of a funeral parlour. It wasn't helped by the oppressive silence. Simply no sound emanated from the rest of the block, not even a toilet flushing or a water pipe dripping. Nothing came up from the street far below. No matter how many times he looked out of the window, no one passed by. The effect was depressing. George was not a depressive by nature but he found himself wishing he was back in the hospital and very soon he began to imagine what if. In particular what if no one ever came back? He looked round frantically. The apartment had no personal items, the sort of thing you might expect a young married couple to have gathered. The kitchen had no special pots and pans, everything looked like the sort of thing you'd expect a landlord to provide. There were no herb dishes, no teapot, no his and her type towels, no paintings, nothing that would tell you a thing about the people who lived there. If he didn't know them they would be opaque to him. He wouldn't even be able to guess their backgrounds. It was the same with the other rooms. The cushions you'd find anywhere; the bedclothes looked like cheap standard issue; the carpets were nylon. There was no washing lying around in the scullery. He opened drawers and found nothing in them, not even a change of underwear. Surely they weren't so poor they only had one set of clothes? Unless he was reading the signs completely wrongly, Tomas and Aldona were two people in transit. They had not yet collected together the baggage of their lives.

Crossing to the living room he opened the bureau. In front of him was the key with the twine on. The key to the one room he wasn't entitled to enter. With a sneer he grabbed it and approached the door. As if suspecting his intentions and determined to look out for its absent owners, the dog had plucked up the courage to move from beneath the table and take up sentry outside the door. It bared its teeth at him as he approached. "Bog off!" he threatened, aiming another kick at it. Discretion got the better of valour and it scuttled away. He laughed but it crossed his mind how peculiar it was that it had tried in its inept way to protect the forbidden citadel. He wondered just what was in there. Well he'd soon know. For a moment he stood outside the bedroom door listening as if someone might be inside. He felt the tension transmitted through the hairs on the nape of his neck. "Stupid prat!" he said and put the key in the door.

Still, he had the feeling of intruding into an inner sanctum, a holy of holies, rather as if he were defiling a shrine. Once inside the buzzing, like a beehive in his head, cleared. What had he expected to find? Some evidence of a secret life? Something like witchcraft? It was a perfectly ordinary room, there was nothing to distinguish it at all. There was a double bed, a wardrobe and a chest of drawers. He began to go through the drawers. Wonder of wonders! Now here was something different, something altogether strange. Photographs of Aldona and Tomas when they were younger. Then, in the middle of this little library of past experiences, he came across something which made his blood tingle: photos of Aldona in more provocative poses, wearing all kinds of unusual, almost theatrical costumes. They were revealing, sexy, soft porn photos. Not only did she appear sometimes almost naked, she was also tied up. She had a thick, plaited rope round her neck and it hung down and covered her otherwise naked breasts, the same ones he had grappled with earlier. She had bonds round her waist, padlocked at the crotch. Her hands stretched out, as if she was begging to be free. The images of bondage sent his hormones into ferment. Who would have believed it? These people had seemed so ordinary and here was evidence that they were the biggest swingers in town. Maybe they had nothing to pique their interest in these places so they spent their time dreaming up more and more bizarre sex games. No wonder his hostess had been up for it! She probably did it with all the lodgers but did Tomas know? The evidence suggested a yes: the photo was taken with a Polaroid; next to it was one of Tomas. He was standing and looking serious, like a total dickhead. It wasn't proof he knew but what would it be doing there if he didn't know what it was accompanying?

George shook his head and blew out in exasperated fashion. He looked again at the photo of Aldona. "Wild!" He licked his lips. He liked anything off the wall. He turned past the photos of Aldona and nearly staggered. There was another picture of a woman in bondage but this wasn't Aldona. The woman wore an eye mask but he recognised the high cheekbones, and even the hour-glass figure, even though her dark hair, this time, was tied in a ponytail. Her arms were stretched out and tied to the wall. She was helpless, just waiting to be exploited, and gagging for it by the tongue protruding from between her large, luscious lips. He just knew it was Zoya.

What had he stumbled on? Putting the photos back in their place, trying desperately to make it look as if he had not disturbed them, he scanned the book shelves but he couldn't understand any Lithuanian so he couldn't tell what the titles were. He pulled out one book. The cover told him that it was a book on Lithuanian mythology. He remembered the talk with the doctor. What had he said about dreaming of the Lithuanian devil? No, he didn't say that exactly. He suddenly felt so claustrophobic he had to get out. The dog looked at him suspiciously as he closed the bedroom door. He looked down at the ground and to each side of the door to see if there was any sign of broken thread, thinking his hosts might have laid a tell-tale for an unwary voyeur. He couldn't see anything.

He went and hammered on the doors again, front and back. He opened a window and he yelled into the courtyard below. Now he wasn't even looking to escape, or for Tomas or Aldona to be warned of his predicament. He was searching only for contact. He felt like Robinson Crusoe. The problem was no one was there. It was like a ghost town. No one heard his cries, nobody answered the knocking. Was everyone in Lithuania out to lunch? After a while he stopped trying to get a response, convincing himself that this was yet another reason why he was right not to do this deal. "As soon as that bastard gets home," he said, "I'm going to insist he takes me to the airport!"

So, when Tomas got in much later it was to a very angry guest. "What the hell are you trying to do?" he raved.

"What do you mean?" Tomas asked innocently.

"Your bloody dozy wife locked me in!" he shouted.

"Did she? That's not like her. She must have had something very large on her mind!" Tomas had a slightly amused grin on his face, as if he found the whole episode funny - or knew something he shouldn't.

George's mouth twisted. "Don't you screw with me!" he shouted, gesticulating wildly at the younger man, who put his hands up to his head as if to ward off blows, but he didn't look that phased as he backed away grinning genially.

"George, George," he said patiently, "it must have been a simple accident! Why would Aldona want to lock you in? She probably just did the same as she always does when she leaves the house. She just forgot we had a visitor, forgot you were here. Strange I agree, as you have made such a big impression on her. Maybe she had something on her mind? Let's ask her together when she gets back, shall we? I'm sure there is a rational explanation. Let's try and hold it together and not be so accusing, shall we?" His calm, reasoning voice quelled George's growing paranoia. He crumpled like a punctured balloon when Tomas produced the key from the wall just round the corner where they hung the coats. "Maybe you just missed them?" he said. "Maybe the coats were covering them and you didn't think to look behind?"

"I'm sure it wasn't there when I looked," George lied but in a crestfallen voice, because he couldn't actually remember if he'd looked round the corner. He was deflated, like anyone faced with an irrational situation and the voice of reason on the other side.

"Okay, it's my fault, I should have mentioned where we kept the spare," Tomas said soothingly, "but let's not blame Aldona. She has a tough enough life as it is. And you, too, you must still be in quite a state. I bet you've had too much excitement for one day?"

He said it with all the appearance of innocence, but George looked at him half suspicious, half afraid. Did he know? He decided to ignore it, not confront it. "I was worried when I couldn't get out," he snivelled. "There could have been a fire or anything." He knew how lame it sounded. He could hear as he said it, sounding like a tosser. "And your bloody phone wasn't working, so I couldn't ring my office!"

"Is it not?" Tomas went across to it, picked up the receiver and said, "You're right, I must report the fault to the telephone company. But you have your cell phone? "

"I told you! Battery's flat," George moaned.

"Of course you did," Tomas replied reassuringly. He clapped his head as if he'd forgotten.

"Dunno why. I've hardly used it!"

"Well, it's not been charged for a while, has it? You will have used it before the flight and then you came here and you went straight out so it's used up all its juice."

"I guess so. I didn't bring a charger, thought I wouldn't need it."

Tomas nodded sympathetically. "So you poor chap, you've been in all alone without any means of communicating. Terrible. Your introduction to my country has been so terrible and I wanted it to go so well. Ah, me!"

He clapped his forehead again so that George suddenly

felt sorry for him instead of the other way round. "Oh, don't blame yourself."

"I'm sorry about it all, George. I wanted things to go so well for you, for you to be impressed with us and the way we do things."

"It's okay, kid, it's okay."

"But I do hope Aldona took good care of you before she left?" There it was again, the body blow. He flushed, feeling guilty and knew he looked it. Tomas was scrutinising him carefully. "She did, didn't she? She took good care of all your needs?"

Was it George's imagination or did he appear to emphasise the word all? He was flustered as he replied. "Oh, yes, oh yes, no problem, she looked after me very well."

"Good," Tomas beamed, "she is a very good, dutiful wife."

"She certainly is," George replied, "yes, you can say that again."

He breathed a sigh of relief as Tomas seemed to accept that as a compliment and then, as if as an afterthought, he added: "George, good news, I was able to send off the deposit today, it will be in your bank now but it is probably too late for you to check that. You will be able to confirm first thing in the morning. I will take you out to a phone myself if this one is still not working or you can use my cell."

George's whole demeanour changed. From the hard-done-by whinger he metamorphosed into the City gent, cheered by the news on the Rialto. "That is good news," he enthused, and he pumped the surprised Tomas's hand. "Excellent!" he exclaimed, "five hundred big ones, right?"

"Five per cent, just like we agreed," Tomas said. "Like you Great Britons, we Lithuanians always keep our word."

George was suddenly back in control. He was the spider in the web again. The fly had landed. He could turn the screw a little himself now. "Hmmm, but you didn't tell me about Zoya, did you?"

"Zoya?" Tomas walked through to the kitchen.

"Yes, Zoya! You said she was Aldona's sister, not yours!"

"Actually, I think I said or intended to day she was Aldona's sister-in-law."

"Who calls their sister, their wife's sister-in-law? It's a weirdo thing to say!"

"Well, you will have to excuse my facility with your language, George, but, even so, I think, unless it is different in the UK, that means there was no word of a lie."

"Well, it's weird if you ask me."

"This is not a subject I wish to discuss, George."

"Well, maybe yous'll have no choice, because your missus says she's coming here tonight and then we will be able to talk."

"We'll leave it till then, shall we?" Tomas replied coolly.

George was taken aback. He had expected angry denials, so he could take pleasure in proving to Tomas he'd lied, but he'd just owned up. "Tomas, what the hell are you up to?"

He was about to repeat the warning about not messing with him when there was a transaction like this in the wings but now he knew the transaction was underway he thought he'd best wait and check the money really was in the bank. There was more than one way of skinning a cat. In fact it could be turned to his use as even more justification for nicking their money, the stupid bastards. He couldn't leave now the deal was almost in the bag. Strange, because earlier he'd not only been willing to light out and write it off, he'd been desperate to get out of here by any means possible. Anyway, he was intrigued. Maybe he should see Zoya, just to satisfy his own curiosity that it was the same woman. A sixth sense tugged at him, though, told him he should get out of there, that this was something off the wall and whacky, incestuous even, something he didn't really want to get mixed up in. But he put all this fear of the future down to nerves, the events of the past few days. After all he'd never been scared of anything in his life, had he? What could a few bloody poverty-stricken Balts do to a ferocious creature like him? How bad could it be?

"Up to?" Tomas replied. "Nothing. You will see why I do not wish to talk about this when you meet Zoya."

"I'm looking forward to that."

Tomas smiled. "Look on my works, ye mighty, and despair."

George hadn't quite caught that, the delivery was so fast. "What did you say?" he asked.

"A work of beauty beyond compare," Tomas repeated.

Before George could question him further, Aldona arrived home. She was breathless, the lift had broken down, she explained, and she had a large bag of shopping which she'd brought up ten flights of stairs. "Oh, poor dear," Tomas said, taking the bag off her.

147

"But, good news! George said you looked after him very well this morning!" He gave her a meaningful glance.

George blushed as she looked at him. He didn't know where to put himself. There was still something knowing in Tomas's look but, cool as cucumber, Aldona replied, "yes, I did, he was very good, easy to take care of."

"Oh yeah that's me," George said a little too enthusiastically, "nobody has to put themself out for me, I'm a doddle to have around."

"Oh, do tell me what you did for him?" Tomas said, a delighted grin on his handsome face."

"Oh I made his breakfast!"

"Oh great!" Tomas held up his hands as if in rapture.

"And made him comfortable!"

"Oh, splendid!"

"And you locked me in!" George intervened. Forced laughter at from the pair of them left him realising this was a good moment to make himself scarce. He complained of tiredness and went to lie down in his room.

"I will go out and report the telephone breakdown," Tomas shouted.

"And the lift breakdown!" Aldona shouted in response. They were shouting in English for his benefit.

Overhearing this from his room, George thought, what a bloody country! Everything was always breaking down. Then he thought about his own experiences to date. Including me, his brain added.

CHAPTER 11

It wasn't like George to be nervous - before he'd come to Lithuania that is - but ever since it had been confirmed that Zoya was coming to dinner he'd been on tenterhooks. He couldn't settle, he was irritable, even the likelihood that the deal had gone through and his bank was now in possession of a large sum of Lithuanian litas couldn't fill him with enthusiasm. He tried to analyse it. He wasn't even sure this was the same woman and yet he had a feeling. It was odd, as if some things were meant to be and he had no control over them. Tomas and Aldona were treating it like a big deal as well, going round sprucing the place up, putting out flowers. Tomas was tetchy. He was doing it against his will but you'd think it was royalty visiting rather than Aldona's sister-in-law. He still hadn't got over that description or Tomas's apparent coldness towards his sister. Was that because he was ashamed of the fact she was a hooker as well as a doctor? If she was; and, if she was, why was she? And was there always this grand production every time she came?

Aldona's attitude to him was off-hand as well. He'd tried a couple of times to goose her whenever Tomas's gaze was averted. Once when Tomas had gone to the loo he'd tried to kiss her and squeeze her tits from behind, reminding her with soft words and his hardness

151

up against her buttocks of the fantastic sex they'd had that morning, but she wasn't responsive. She wasn't hostile; she just treated him like one of the family, part of the furniture. She even gave him jobs to do in honour of Zoya's imminent arrival but there was no expression of intimacy. She neither stopped his attempts to molest her nor encouraged them. "Come on," he said to her once in exasperation as, kneading her backside while she carefully peeled potatoes, she gave no sign of being distracted from her task, "you know you just love it!" But she was back into that me-no-understand-English routine, which he found aggravating because she knew much more than she was letting on. It must be a confidence thing, he decided.

Tomas breezed around complacently, nuzzling his wife from time to time - it was sickening for George to watch, particularly as he did get some reaction! He was jealous and wanted to be the centre of attention. He could have smashed Tomas's face in, he seemed so arrogant, so pleased with himself. He wanted to say, Tomas, your wife needs a man, I gave her the fuck of her life this morning while you were out at work, you dipstick, but he kept his counsel. A malicious thought was however forming in his mind. He would save that one until he was just about to get on the plane. He could see the stunned look on the jerk's face even now as he sauntered off through the immigration channels. He was so proper and correct and steeped in fear of Eastern European regimes that he wouldn't even have the passion to do something out of the ordinary like give chase into the illegal area of the airport and plant him one. That's why his wife needed a red-blooded man, not the anaemic, effeminate wimp she'd married.

When he thought about this airport endgame scenario he was happier in himself; he'd make the bastard squirm for treating him like an inferior. That's how it was with Tomas. Everything the Brits could do the Lithuanians could do better, that was his perspective. It hadn't sunk in that this was a Third World country coming to terms with the end of the Cold War. He actually believed they were ready to take their place at the top table with the developed nations of the world. The preferred E.C status had gone to his head more than most of his countrymen. George was careful not to get too carried away with these thoughts. He mustn't let the mask slip. This guy and his colleagues had to think they were future business partners or a wheel might come off, even at this stage.

Jesus he was dusting a sideboard! "The things I do for the company!" The company! No sooner had he uttered those words than he was thinking of his mates, Marty and Fred and Dougie and Joe. Wait till he told them what had happened here. Their eyes would pop out of their heads. Maybe they didn't always approve of the way he got things done, but most of that was jealousy, because they weren't the type adventures happen to. They were too busy protecting their stash to take a chance; jumped up accountants. The worst was Joe, he was the most careful, but what could you expect from a guy who'd got his seed capital from a European lottery win? That was all that had got him into the bank. He had no other credentials. "Me and Marty should have taken him, too," he began telling himself in the bathroom mirror, noticing his morning's shave was no longer so smooth. It wasn't too late to take him even now, just when the bastard thought he'd got his feet under the table! He decided to put that one on his and Marty's hidden agenda the next time they met for a divi up. George didn't like Joe's silent, accusatory looks, as if he thought him a loose cannon. "Fuck you!" he said to the mirror and the imaginary Joe. He was also jealous of the ease with which their new partner had come across his pile. He'd had to make his money the hard way, out of old peoples' homes, before the government got over-regulatory. He'd sold out because there was no money in it anymore. It had nothing to do with that time Mrs. Thompson checked out in the Christmas pudding and they'd almost closed one of his homes, but he'd seen the writing on the wall then. They'd even wanted to see all the old women's wills, just to check if anything had been left to him! The cheek of it.

Now he and Marty went back a long way and Marty was well-connected, by which he meant mob-connected. He'd made his money out of the doors and the bandits. It used to be sixpences, now it was pound coins. Christ, he could remember the graft emptying the spare van loads of them back in the old days when he'd just got started in the business. The thing about this investment banking compared to that was it was so sanitised, you got an introduction into high society just because you called yourself an investment banker and they were all over you like flies on an open jugular. The higher up in society the more they'd do for money. The women would take their knickers off, the blokes would too if you were that way inclined, which he'd never been of course. Those society blokes would pimp you for their women, for their wives even; they'd lavish entertainment on you at their country houses, and it always ended up in an orgy. Yes, it had its compensations being an investment banker.

But the things he did for the company! Marty had tried to justify it, he was thinking, as he dabbed aftershave on his face, by saying, "but you're the best salesman among us, Georgie, you're the one who can close a deal. That's what he was, a closer, the coolest closer there ever was and now here he was, sweating at the armpits because he was about to meet the night doctor! What was wrong with him! "It's got to be love!" he said, grinning at himself, but that wasn't possible. Love was a momentary thing. It was giving Aldona one this morning and then he didn't think about her until he wanted the next one. He couldn't even remember the bonk with the night doctor, and yet for him to wake up tied up in a cold bath? Jesus that must have been some night! He emerged from the bathroom to find Tomas dressing for dinner. "This girl must be a celebrity," George said with a huge grin.

"Oh no, George, I am not staying," Tomas replied, "I have another engagement." George was put out. He'd seen Tomas busying himself with the preparations and now he wasn't staying! "You see, George, she's bringing a Russian with her. He was the commander of the occupying forces in the Baltic region. I'm afraid it is against my principles to eat with this man. He was guilty of many atrocities when he was here. Many people disappeared. Oh, he's a hero now all right, because of how he behaved when it was all up for the Russians. But I am not fooled. I know he was just trying to save his own skin then. There was no love for my people in what he did. He was on the run and making the best of it!" He made a clapping sound with his hands as if to emphasise the suddenness of the tanks' departure, then he continued, "I do not want him in my home even, but on this I have no choice because it is Aldona's home too and she hopes this is serious, she hopes she will be able to do some match-making here, you know what it's like with the women, don't you?" He laughed and slapped George playfully. "Here!" he added, and he was pouring a whisky into a crystal glass from a crystal decanter, neither of which George could remember seeing when he'd done his trawl through their belongings. "Dutch courage you say, don't you?"

"Hey, steady on!" Tomas was not ungenerous. "There must be four fingers there. You having one?"

"Oh no, not me, I have to drive."

Again George was thrown slightly off balance but he didn't want to show it. He sipped happily at the whisky. It was quality stuff. He tried to make small talk. "So, is it serious between your sis and this general guy? Not sure I've ever met a real life general. Is he the real deal or a mickey-mouse one like those South Americans?"

"Oh, he was the real deal, all right. Very powerful man in the Soviet Union. As for Zoya...." He shrugged. "I don't know."

"Oh, really?" George replied, "well, if this Russian is the wannabe bridegroom, he's going to have his hands full with that one, that's all I can say, if she's the girl I think she is...."

"George, I've told you not even to think that, it is impossible. No way, I tell you." He was throwing his hands out by his side in exaggerated dismissal of an idea which was repugnant to him. "Zoya is a saint. Why, she is coming here to celebrate a big donation given to the children's ward at her hospital!"

"But you're not going to be there for her!"

"That, I tell you, is by the by. It is nothing to do with it. I do not approve of this Russian liaison, that's all. Anyway, you have the wrong person, she is not the kind of woman to get involved in things like that."

"Like what?" George asked, feigning innocence, but he was thinking, like your wife isn't? Just like that?

"She is not, I tell you." George was grinning. He just loved winding these Eastern Europeans up. They had no sense of humour, they took life so seriously. Tomas sniffed. "You will know that as soon as you meet her. It is impossible I tell you."

"Okay it's impossible," George agreed, but he decided to tease Tomas some more. "Don't run away with the idea saints don't like sex," he said, "even Princess Di needed a man or two in her life. These girls with a lot of saintly energy often have their earthly values as well, they like it up them as much as any lass from the mean streets. Take your missus now, Tomas, she's a lively lady, isn't she, butter wouldn't melt in her mouth? But I bet once she gets you between the sheets she's a little tigress, isn't she? I bet she can't get enough of the old Lithuanian pork sword?"

Tomas looked embarrassed but at the same time he seemed half-pleased by the suggestion that he was something of a stud. "You wouldn't ask me to comment on that, would you George?" He grinned nervously.

"No need, no need," George replied, "You told me everything last night." He enjoyed the look of resentment on Tomas's face as he flinched at the thought he'd poured out his soul to this total stranger who was showing every sign of turning it to his own advantage. Sometimes you just had to accept you'd played the wrong piece, boxed yourself in. George went on with a wink, "I know women, take it from me. I know your little lady might look like a petal but she'll jump the fences with you if you give her the chance. She's a good girl her. Look after her! She's the type who'd stand in the dock with you, precious them."

"Yes, thanks for the advice, George."

"Don't you mention it, mate!"

George bantered away with Tomas enthusiastically, even forgiving him for deserting them, but he noticed when he took time off and got back to his room he was feeling sweaty. He'd succeeded in working himself up whilst extolling Aldona's charms, and the main dish was yet to be served! All his earlier fears had dissipated now. He couldn't understand why he'd got himself so paranoid. Tomas didn't know his arse from his elbow.

The idea that someone as wet behind the years as Tomas could have been setting up an artful dodger like George was just plain preposterous. The latter was licking his lips at the prospects for the rest of the evening. He just had that old feeling, that instinct almost, that there was something here for him. When had he last thought that? Oh, yes, the Club Indigo. But that was the past and this was the now. More fool Tomas if he didn't want to be there to see the fireworks. Some people just had no idea how to get a life.

CHAPTER 12

No one seemed to know precisely when Zoya would arrive but it was noticeable how the tension in the household increased as the time ticked by, or, George wondered, was he simply imagining that because he could feel the pressure increase inside himself? He didn't know why. Should he be phased at the possibility of at last getting an explanation for his lost night? He was owed it, wasn't he?

There he was listening desultorily to a conversation between Tomas and Aldona, which seemed to become more and more heated, so that even the dog slunk off to hide. He pricked up his ears every time he heard Zoya's name but it was clear from the number of times she crept into the conversation and the way their passions seemed to rise at each mention that Tomas and Aldona were in some disagreement about her coming or, more likely from what Tomas had said, about the general's accompanying her. What was it to Tomas, he was thinking? It's not as if he was out there in the trenches, the Lithuanian partisan fighting the invader from the east!

As he listened he guessed Aldona was trying to persuade him to stay but Tomas was having none of it, he was adamant. Finally he flatly forced his hands outward and away from his body and shouted, "ne, ne!"

in response to Aldona's pleas. That meant no in anyone's language, George guessed, and he realised the climax had arrived and following it there was flat calm. Aldona shrugged and, amusingly, at least as George perceived it, walked away sticking one finger up in the air. Good for you lass, he thought and he had to admit his trousers gave him a pinch at that moment as if reminding him that there were other tensions also which needed some release. But those gestures were universal, he was thinking. And whatever else could be said of the mystery lady, she obviously aroused immense passions. He remembered the photos in the secret room and wondered how Tomas felt about those as he poured George another glass, then, even as he toasted his guest, he, strangely and rather disinterestedly, picked up his coat and left. George did a double-take at the haste of it all and just wondered suddenly if he had a cute little mistress waiting for him. He'd heard all the excuses but he'd made them himself and the one that usually explained his absence from domestic duties was not quite as high-faluting as his host might want to make out, although it was usually work-connected. He strolled into the passage, where Aldona smiled at him bravely. "Where's he going?" He pretended to be mystified as if Tomas had said nothing to him.

"He forgot he have appointment," Aldona replied.

"What?" George exclaimed and he looked at his watch. He acted as if Tomas had never confided in him his reasons for making himself scarce. "Are you kidding?

An appointment? But Zoya's coming!" He said it as if it should have been the most important event in Tomas's life.

"Yes, she is, " Aldona replied a trifle mournfully, or so it seemed, but then she sidled up to George and, as if confiding in an old friend, said, "he's terrified of her, he can't stay where she is for long."

George looked bewildered. "Terrified, why? She's his sister!" But Aldona squeezed his fingers and that touch communicated itself straight to his groin. He held out his free hand to take her by the hip but she just breezed off as if there was nothing more to be said and that momentary and very intimate if innocent contact was all he was going to get. It was enough to set him thinking, though, that he might be in if Tomas was out late. After a few drinks Aldona's defences might be down, her resolution less firm. He downed his whisky and poured himself another. Dutch courage! That's what Tomas had called it.

It was some time later that the doorbell rang and George sat, pretending to read the English newspaper, which Tomas had very thoughtfully brought back for him that evening. There were voices in the hall. Hastily he dried the palms of his hands on his trousers. It wasn't like him to sweat like this. You'd think it was the Caribbean or somewhere hot, anywhere other than North East Europe with the winter approaching.

Hearing shrieks of laughter in the hall, really raucous female stuff like at a hen party with the cheap chardonnay flowing free, he stepped to the living room door and looked out, still sipping from his glass. A bizarre sight met his eyes. Aldona was holding out the key on the twine and a man was dutifully intoning indecipherable words, no doubt swearing on every woman he'd ever had seven times sideways that he wasn't going to enter the holy of holies. George couldn't help the frisson of alarm which wriggled its way down his spine. "Fucking hell!" he muttered and he clapped his forehead with his open palm. The group in the hall hadn't even noticed him, so engrossed were they in their bizarre pantomime. Another woman, presumably Zoya, tall and elegant but with her back to him and showing beautiful, shapely, dark-stockinged legs with the seam totally straight, was standing with a flash camera taking pictures. She had a headscarf round her hair and he could see none of it, whether it was short, long, dark, fair. She stood with her back to him and snapped away happily. That wasn't going to be for long, however, and the butterflies made his stomach churn as the thought struck him: *let's have a look at you before you see me!*

The man took the key, entered one room then exited again, moved into a second room then turned round and held up his hands like a monkey and grinned. It had to be the general but he acted like a puppet on a string. Moments later, he handed back the key, smiling politely and saying some more words. If what Tomas had said was correct this was a former commander of the Red Army for Christ's sake! The two women exchanged raucous comments, maybe even blue ones he thought, his imagination running wild because of those raunchy pics.

The general seemed to join in the occasion without any sign of self-consciousness as if it was perfectly natural that he should take part in this ritual. The women cajoled him to enter more rooms but he seemed to think that unnecessary. He smiled but each time he put up his hand and shook his head. George wished he'd been this calm and authoritative in his refusal instead of losing his rag. Zoya gave one last shriek of laughter and disappeared into Aldona's bedroom. Aldona followed her in dramatic fashion, like a Vanessa Redgrave fleeing a gang bang. She turned round to the general and said, "ne! ne!" forbidding him entry with another giggle. George suspected that a hurried conflab was about to take place about him but he tried to ignore it. He slunk back into the living room, hoping his voyeurism hadn't been noticed.

The general came through then to the same room and did not seem surprised to see him there. He spoke a little English and there was that embarrassing moment when, without the girls there, they tried to find something in common and the best George could come up with was Margaret Thatcher. This broke the ice because it turned out the general had met her once when she visited the USSR. He'd had dinner with her - and about two thousand others, George guessed. George had met her too. She'd once presented him with an award for Entrepreneur of the Year. A friend of the investment community was Maggie! Actually he'd quite fancied giving her one too, even if she was a bit past her sell by date. It was that thing about powerful women. He tried to tell the general that but, if he understood, he just grinned politely. There was George telling this Russian soldier about how he reckoned Maggie was secretly partial to the old pork sword and he was grinning and nodding his head as if he knew it was right. "Iron lady," he was saying, "iron lady!" and he was thumbing his nose as if that had some significance.

George was still trying to work out that remark when, after what seemed like an eternity, Zoya made an entrance and there was yet another surprise. She was now hiding behind a Venetian mask. The general called out with delight and George just looked gobsmacked. So thrown was he by the gesture and what it might mean, although it could of course be pure coincidence, that it took him a few moments to realise that this woman had blond hair, and, not only that, but it was a knot of thick curls. Behind the mask also he could see that she was wearing spectacles and when she stood sideways to him they bore the name *Dior* on the arm. He didn't know whether he was disappointed or not but the pendulum had swung back in favour of this being a mere coincidence. He was secretly disappointed but, at the same time, he would have professed himself relieved, so tangled up were his emotions about this meeting. It was as if he was about to be confronted with something about himself he didn't really want to know.

Aldona followed her sister-in-law and she was also carrying a Venetian mask in front of her face. He wondered if she emulated everything Zoya did. She seemed pleased to see him there and she bounced up to him joyfully and took away the mask momentarily before putting it back in place so that he found himself, instead of staring into her eyes, looking straight down her cleavage even as her right hand was caressing his cheek with the tips of her slender fingers. Suddenly he sensed he was on a promise, whichever way the night turned out, and that gave him a lift. "George," Aldona continued, "this is Tomas's sister Zoya, "I'm not sure you've met, although you may have seen her at the hospital."

Now Zoya dropped the mask, and she did it without hesitation and with a delightful smile, while she held out her hand rather formally to shake his. Strangely, he found himself looking at the ground; he couldn't look her straight in the eye. He was aware of long, long legs, the type that went right up through the pantyhose, and he couldn't escape the secret wonder if he'd been there. The thought added to the fact that he just couldn't make eye contact. It was as if he was afraid that she would know immediately what he was thinking. Then, Aldona was handing the cocktails around and everyone was speaking in Lithuanian and, after that first mumbled exchange in which Zoya had held out her hand to him and said in English, "pleased to meet you," he still hadn't been able to meet her glance.

She flitted around now sometimes holding up the mask, sometimes not, Aldona following suit like she was her little understudy. It was bewildering because he could never get a good look at her. As she moved around he did, however, catch the fragrance of her perfume and it hit him right where it hurts. He was able to steal a look at her from the other side of the group. The Dior glasses were big and round, enormous. The disguise, if it was one, worked. He couldn't really swear it was the same woman and now the image in the photographs was getting in the way too. She had the same high, maybe they were Slavonic, cheekbones, and big, slightly protruding lips but her hair was not black and long and tied back as the bar girl's had been, it was a mass of rich, blond curls, and her complexion seemed lighter. Yet they were of the same build, tall and willowy with great figures, the bosom full and high, not matronly, the hips pronounced, the gait loose from the pelvis.

Their demeanours were different but so were the circumstances: the other girl had been brooding, more cynical perhaps, negotiating a trick, where this Zoya was effervescent, overflowing with joy, or so it seemed. He noticed for the first time that the general was gazing at her admiringly and he knew instinctively, in the sense that it takes one to know one, that he was hoping for a bit more than conversation tonight. That gave him a pang of jealousy and he wondered if he'd be thinking of the other woman as he was screwing Aldona tonight. And what if Tomas came home and found them on the job? Or, worse still, he came home before they clocked on?

Suddenly he was trying to concentrate on something the general was saying to him, vaguely conscious that Zoya had Aldona in raptures with some story she was telling, and it suddenly dawned on him that, since the initial greeting, they'd talked in their own language and it might as well have been double Dutch as far as he was concerned. Despite the general's present attempts in his broken English, he was uncomfortable as they sat down to dinner because, although Aldona had paid lip service to the need to bring him into the conversation, he understood suddenly that he was surplus to requirements. They insisted on talking in their own language. From time to time Zoya glanced across at him surreptitiously but the look seemed more what-on-earth's-he-doing-here than I-want-you-you-gorgeous-hunk-of-man. He decided to try and intervene and get a word in edgeways but he wished she'd take off the poser specs.

It was all so surreal he had to pinch himself to remind him that he actually was in Lithuania, that strange things were going on and he'd better not lose concentration. He wished he hadn't drunk as much whisky now because his sense weren't sharp. He was disappointed with Zoya, too, because he'd been sure he would have known her and now he felt like someone at a Police identification parade who'd caught a fleeting glimpse of a suspect and was being asked to make a firm identification but couldn't be sure it was the same person. It was well-nigh impossible. Whatever cocktail he'd imbibed that night had played havoc with his constitution and clouded his memory and he was guzzling the wine now like it had gone out of fashion. A momentary black out, after which the room swam back into vision, made him realise he'd best slow down.

Anyway since that night Zoya had assumed mythical proportions and her image had been disturbed in the process. The fact she was Tomas's sister didn't help either because it had to be said they had similar characteristics. It is astonishing how alike some people look, he thought. There were lots of people George had been told he looked like: Crocodile Dundee, for instance, and a famous football manager. When he analysed it, and he had plenty of time to as they studiously ignored him, he realised there are only so many types in the world. He was disappointed but he had to accept that Zoya 1 and Zoya 2 could be one massive coincidence. Like Tomas had implied, it was a common enough name in this part of the world. "Hey," he said, and all four of them turned and looked at him, appearing momentarily surprised that he had opened his mouth. "I heard you'd had some good luck?" He was looking pointedly at Zoya now, belying his earlier reluctance to catch her eye. They looked at him expectantly waiting for him to finish and he suddenly felt self-conscious so he blurted the next bit out. "You know, Tomas was saying your hospital came into a windfall?"

"Windfall?" Zoya said and he could see the vocabulary had evaded her.

"A donation," he said, "a gift? A surprise perhaps?"

Zoya's face creased into a smile and he was struck suddenly by the fact it was her. That's the kind of thing no plastic surgery could hide. But it was like a light flashing on and then it went off again and all was darkness once more. But she didn't speak, it was the general who spoke: "Ah yes," he said and he grinned and tried to make it sound funny that he did all of a sudden speak some English. "That's just what we were talking about."

"I didn't know that," George replied icily, "I don't speak your language."

"Sorry, Georgi of course you don't," Aldona said and he cast a sharp glance at her. People were always calling him that. It was like a private joke and it was beginning to grate.

Zoya leapt in with, "yes, we were, we were talking about St. George's. We named it after our patron saint because just like you and your country the UK, Georgi, our patron saint is St. George. Were you named after this great hero, Georgi?"

"Hey, kid, I don't know," he replied and he was
conscious of the general smirking away in the
background, no doubt thinking how could this English
businessman be confused with some great Mediaeval
hero and he was resentful of that. But the thought came
mixed with his memories of the back street in
Scotswood in which he was born just after the days
when it had ceased to be Scotswood-on-Tyne and had
been subsumed in the city of Newcastle and the truth is
he was born on the mean streets but that didn't mean he
couldn't be a hero too.

His chin jutted out and he was about to amplify his
words when Zoya spoke soothingly, perhaps noticing
his sudden distress if he had communicated that (had he
because he was usually so poker-faced?). "It is terrible
that we forgot you, how terribly ill-mannered of us,
we've been ignoring Georgi, forgetting he couldn't
speak Lithuanian." But even then she made it sound
like it was a crime, like just about the whole world and
his dog spoke this obscure Baltic language which
Tomas, in one of his pseudo-intellectual moments, had
explained to him had the same Indo-European origins
as English but that's just about where the similarity
ended. Then, rather sarcastically, she ended by adding,
"And I can see Georgi is used to being the centre of
attention." The way she said his name didn't escape
him and there was a nuance in it too. It didn't sound
unkind but he knew he was being taken down a peg or

two.

Not content with that, Zoya took up the story with what turned out to be her own brand of sparkling good humour. She told the general she was going to tell the tale in English for Georgi's benefit and he nodded modestly. It seemed that some time ago before the liberation the hospital had treated the general's son when he'd had an accident in Vilnius. The kid was near death but miraculously the hospital had brought him back to life. Zoya had been finishing her training then and she'd been working in surgery that night so she'd helped Dr. Pilkauskas, who'd since retired, to save the kid's life. "No, no, you're too modest!" the general exclaimed, leaving George wondering why he'd not shown the same facility with English in one to one conversation. Maybe he was more comfortable in a group with others for whom it was a second language than addressing someone directly who was a native speaker.

Anyway, Zoya went on, more or less ignoring the interruption: the general was really grateful and he'd said he was going to come back one day and repay them for all they'd done but they'd all gone yeah yeah, they all say that. Big cheese, big promises, big let-down, like politicians everywhere. Ha ha. Then after the breakup of the USSR the general went into business. Zoya made the sign of inverted commas in the air and George and Aldona guffawed with laughter because they knew she meant the protection racket. The general was looking mildly amused because he didn't appear to appreciate he was the butt of that joke. Maybe his English wasn't up to that much despite his outburst a few moments before. Maybe, like he'd observed of Aldona, he didn't hear it as well as he spoke it. George shook his head, partially to clear it but partially also because you couldn't tell with these Balts: they should be further back than the Chinese but they were cleverer than you gave them credit for. He hadn't thought about it but he was suddenly enjoying the intimacy of being part of the charmed circle whilst someone else was excluded. And Zoya was a fascinating narrator. The general had kept a regiment and a tank or two as a retirement present to himself, that's how it seemed to work in the USSR. But he'd been as good as his word, he'd come back and given them a donation of a cool two million bucks, U.S not litas. "Putting the profits of gangland to good use, eh?"

"So why didn't you call it after the general? " George asked. "Why use St. George? " He said it almost proudly as if it were an ancestor of his they were honouring.

"Ah well," Zoya replied, "that would have been so nice but some of my countrymen are not quite so ready for that yet. Even my brother ...." Her voice tailed off and she suddenly looked sad.

George didn't let on that he knew but asked, "So what happened to the boy, was he okay?"

The mood suddenly became more sombre. "Well, that's it," Zoya said, "he was okay, but that's half the reason the general came back - because he hadn't before and he thought he'd been punished for breaking his promise because his son was killed in the Russian army, in Chechnya. He was only nineteen."

"Aaah!" There was a mutual exclamation of sympathy and everyone looked at the general who, this time, had understood only too well.

"Ah, there's an old proverb about a man not escaping his fate!" Zoya sighed. "It's like our ritual, isn't it Aldona?" George felt slightly unnerved by the reintroduction of this theme. "It stems from an ancient folk-tale about a prince who was warned never to go in a certain room in his wife's castle. What did he do?"

"Don't tell me, he disobeyed," George chipped in but he sounded in his own ears like a person in a dream.

"Of course he did, Georgi. And what happened to him?" George just shrugged in a resigned way so on she went. "In the room he met a man, but this was no ordinary man. The difference was he had no *soul*." She paused, letting the word sink in. "Do you know how the soulless man repaid his saviour?"

George shook his head morosely. He didn't know why but it had an awful inevitability about it. "I don't know, kid, but I guess it wasn't good."

"No, it wasn't. He stole everything the prince had. That's what soulless people do, Georgi. I don't need to tell you that, do I?"

George hung on her every word like a person in a trance. "What's that got to do with the general?" he asked. And he was conscious that his voice was thick with drink, not slurring but not far off either. It had caught up on him all of a sudden or it was coming in waves. It occurred to him that whatever he'd had that night wasn't totally out of his system yet..

"It's about fate," she replied. "Both the general and his son had a fate. One was to die young and the other was to lose his son to violence. And to feel responsible for it, to feel he had to atone for it." She was carrying on as if the guy wasn't there.

"Oh I can't swallow that," George responded, "a man is in control of his own fate. Okay, there's things you can do nothing about, accidents and that kind of thing, but the general wasn't responsible for what happened to his son. I don't see why he should take it so personally, he must be very superstitious."

Zoya turned her large spectacles on George. They must have been varifocals, because of the way her eyes opened wide above them as if she were focussing differently, and photochromes or transition lenses because they had turned dark. He had a flash of deja vu, as if she had looked at him that way before, and of course the girl in the bar had. "So you are the master of your fate, the captain of your soul, are you Georgi?" she asked with the first show of the imperiousness he had noticed in the bar room Zoya.

George felt the perspiration standing out on the nape of his neck but he tried not to show it "I think so," he said, but it felt like he had gulped out the words.

"You don't think perhaps it was because his father was a brave soldier that he made his son be the same and so brought him to his death?"

"Well, I can live with the first two of those propositions, kid," he said, trying to sound confident, "but not that one about bringing him to his death. He might just as well have lived."

"Don't you think it was written in the stars that he would die that way, that there was a certain inevitability about it which he could not escape?"

"No, I don't," George said, "there's nothing written in the stars, it all happens by chance."

Zoya appeared to ignore this remark and change tack. "Take you for instance, Georgi, are you married?"

"Separated," he said.

"Divorced?"

"No, not divorced, not yet. She doesn't speak to me, the daughters don't speak to me either, all I do is keep handing over cash." He was pleased at the general's laugh and nod of approval; suddenly it was like they were part of a male conspiracy.

"But don't you feel a responsibility towards your loved ones?" Zoya persisted. "I mean, if something were to happen to them because you were not home to look after them would you not blame yourself?"

"Me? No, why should I blame myself?" He felt uncomfortable with the answer. He knew what he was saying wasn't all true but he felt like he was being forced to play a role, the one he had adopted in life, the suit he had donned of the callous, ruthless businessman, only interested in the pursuit of wealth and material happiness. Was that him? Maybe not, originally, but that original self was a long time ago and he was barely recognisable now. If his old self turned up in his office looking for a job he'd kick him out as someone who'd never make it, not in this world.

The shudder he gave did not escape Zoya. "Because maybe you could have prevented it? What for example if one of your daughters was stalked by a nasty man and attacked and raped....?"

"Zoya!" Aldona exclaimed.

It had no effect. George had no choice but to look straight at her now, pretend he wasn't afraid of this example. "What if that were to happen?" she said, "wouldn't you, as her father, think, I could have prevented that if I'd just looked after her better?"

"No," George said, "I'm a great believer in people being responsible for themselves. You can't blame every misfortune that happens to you on others, or on God or fate or the workings of a cruel universe. It's just not like that. Life is more random than that."

"So you do not believe in God, Georgi?"

"Me, what the hell, no! You're on your own in this life, kid, you might as well get what you can here because you sure aren't going to get it anywhere else. You take it because no bozo's going to give it to you."

"That is a code which would justify any kind of behaviour," Zoya said slowly.

"Yeah, it would, you can do anything as long as you don't get caught," he said, conscious his mouth was running away like a juggernaut and he was unable to stop it but feeling strong, powerful even, in the truth of his belief, "if you're big enough, if you're above the law. The thing that stops most people breaking the law is they're scared to, they're scared of the consequences.

If they could they'd grab everything they could get their hands on so it would ease the passage through this life, but they don't because they're scared they'll lose more by trying. That's why the little people are the most law abiding. They daren't chance their arm because they know they've got no chance of getting away with it."

"And are you one of the little people, Georgi?"

"Me?" George said, his protruding lip curling over slightly, "don't you believe it kid, I'm the king of the jungle! There's nothing out there frightens me. Biggest bastard in the valley, that's me!" Zoya weighed him up. George was gazing at her cockily now. He thought he was passing this test and he got the idea she was warming to him, she liked his manly approach, but he still wondered what was wrong with him, why couldn't he stop? Whether it was the same woman or not was irrelevant. He fancied her. This little exchange had made the blood rush to his groin better than Viagra. He liked intelligent, witty, cynical, beautiful women. Zoya was all of that and she was looking at him as if she thought she might have underestimated him.

Everyone else seemed to be looking at the two of them spellbound, aware of the electricity between them. Eat your heart out Aldona he was thinking, your matchmaking plans are out of the window too. The general was looking, well, alarmed. The temperature had gone up in the room. "So you would not feel at all responsible for a young person you brought into the world and set on their way to goals you had provided for them?" Zoya continued crisply.

He hadn't been prepared for the resumption. He'd thought that phase in their relationship had passed. "Hey, I'm not being taken in by that," George said, "I can see what you're trying to do, but, yes, you have responsibility in law for them till they're eighteen, okay, and you bring them into the world yes, and you give them a certain direction, all right, but you don't provide the goals for them."

"You don't influence them?"

"Hey, again I didn't say that babe! Don't you be putting words in my mouth!" He wagged a finger at her and she smiled as if she knew he had her measure. "You maybe influence them but they make their own decisions ultimately."

"And they are in control always of that decision?"

"No, maybe not, but everyone has to live out his own destiny, no one else can do that for them, who knows what's written up there?"

"Written up where?"

He pointed upwards towards the ceiling but really through it and into the great beyond. "Up there. In the stars!"

Aldona started clapping and laughing uproariously whilst George looked on. He was going redder and redder and trying to work out what she and Zoya found so damn funny. He was trying to remember everything he'd said to see why it sounded ridiculous! But he couldn't get his head round it, his thoughts whirled around like debris caught up in a twister! At last Aldona caught hold of her mirth and, wiping her eyes, said, still chuckling, "it's just that Zoya has trapped you, like she traps everyone sooner or later, I could see it was going to happen and you walked straight into it!"

"Trapped? What yous on about?" George asked incredulously.

"You said before nothing's written up there in the stars, it's all random," Aldona replied with an intelligence and a command of his language which again unnerved George, "but you've just admitted everyone has to live out his own destiny, and now you say who knows what's written up there?"

George was livid. "I didn't know we were playing a game," he said whilst they roared with laughter at his expense. He didn't like being taken for a ride by a woman. He liked them clever and witty and intelligent and cynical and beautiful but preferably knowing their place. Even though they now spoke in English, he remained quiet the rest of the evening except for the odd sporadic flurry of conversation. He had to anyway because Zoya held everyone in thrall with her expositions on her country's history. The Teutonic Knights had been a favourite subject of Tomas's as well he remembered from that interminable car ride when he'd been released from the hospital supposedly into the comfort of a warm bed at home. Zoya seemed to have acquired from somewhere the same enthusiasm for the subject but she had added to it a knowledge of English literature because she explained how Geoffrey Chaucer's knight in *The Knight's Tale* had joined one of their sommer-reysas, the crusades, against her people, as indeed had the real Henry 1V, he who was formerly known as Bolinbroke and was the murderer of Richard 11. She looked at George pointedly as she said this. Quick as a flash, he responded, "don't look at me, kid. I wasn't there."

"Ah, you have an alibi!" This caused hilarity throughout the group. Zoya stared at him, shaking her head in appreciation, but he still couldn't see her face for the damn glasses. He wanted to rip them off and look her straight in the eyes. He wanted to say to her, did you wreck my bed? Why did you tie me up in the bath? But he didn't dare because he wasn't sure and anyway he didn't feel confident enough to go that far. Not yet anyway. But if he got her on her own it might be a different story. Might? No might about it!

A little later Zoya and the general rose to go. George followed them into the corridor. Things hadn't gone exactly to plan and wasn't that always the way with anticipation? But all in all he felt that, after a dodgy start, he'd acquitted himself okay. Outside in the corridor by the lift, which seemed to be back working now, the two women kissed affectionately, Zoya still in her glasses. George shook hands with the general, and then Zoya came towards him to give him a farewell peck. He was momentarily overwhelmed again by her perfume. She kissed his cheek and then she said, "I will see you tomorrow, back here at three o'clock?" Her hand brushed his hip. She spoke in a low voice, and not just so that no one else could hear but also because it was *her* voice, the husky one he remembered. He was thrown totally. Tomas and Aldona would of course be at work then. She would know that.

As she leaned into him he had a sight of her eyes behind the glasses. They were cool and dark, just the way he had seen them in his dreams. "So it was you?" His voice came out as a half croak, like a frog's. "What's with the disguise?"

She looked over her shoulder to where the other three chatted whilst they waited for the newly fixed lift. "Hush," she said, "they'll overhear."

So he had been right. It was a secret life she led. Perhaps they didn't know of it. Perhaps they knew nothing of her in reality. She was an extraordinary woman. "I don't know," he said, "what happened last time?" She laughed and pushed him. Aldona came across and gave a grin. "Come on then, you two, share

184

the joke!" This was the woman who couldn't speak English?

"George was commenting on the ritual," Zoya said. "He thinks we're strange." She drew the vowel out, giving him a malicious grin at the same time.

He felt embarrassed, foolish. Aldona said, "He's right, it's a stupid thing to do. Very kinky, if you ask me." Then she winked at George and that wink spoke volumes. Maybe the night was still young. "But it's a sign of trust," she said, "a sign that you can trust your *hostess* and *she* can trust you!" She emphasised both the feminine noun and pronoun.

"Ah," George said as if he understood.

"You see," Zoya said, "the person with the key is an allegory for the soul. The soul enters into your host's castle. Your host could lock it out but to show you that your soul is always welcome he gives you this key. It is very simple."

"Very simple," George agreed.

"Maggie Thatcher!" the general called to him from across the hall.

"The old pork sabre, son, same to you general," George replied jovially, giving the grinning general the thumbs up.

"You know about the soul, Georgi?" Zoya brought him back to her with another discomforting question. She was the new Zoya again and he found the transition between personae disturbing to say the least.

He decided to be silly. "Oh yeah, Wilson Pickett, you mean, wait till the midnight hour?" He began singing and prancing about until he realised they were looking at him and he was behaving strangely. Rather nervously he stopped in mid-song and mid-prance and looked back at them. He was right; they were looking at him in what could be described as an amused way. "That's very good, Georgi," Zoya said, "I'm sure you've missed your vocation."

They all laughed including a rather crestfallen but still chirpy George. The lift came and with a knowing glance Zoya reminded him without words of their tryst the next day. He nodded secretly and smiled. The lift door closed. He had a momentary vision of her hanging on gaily to the general and thought jealously, he is getting it tonight, the lucky bastard, he's going to be right in there. "Aldona," he called out as if as an afterthought. She yawned and made it clear that if he had anything in mind he could forget it for this evening. Pity, he'd counted on that. He'd wanted it to be Zoya but it looked like the general was the one getting that. Aldona was probably nervous about Tomas showing up when they were on the job. She was looking at him expectantly, waiting for him to finish and he bottled what he was going to ask her but still continued, "what did you mean when you said Zoya specialised in transcendentalism, what is that?"

"Hypnosis," she replied nonchalantly. She turned away without noticing his open mouth. He watched her sway down the corridor and he was in two minds. Just his luck to have a right storker on now because of the way Zoya had wound his DNA up and here was Aldona playing it like little miss muppet but then, also, there were the words ringing in his ear.

It must have been about one in the morning when Tomas came in. Judging by the way he scratched at the lock trying to make the key fit and then lurched noisily down the passage to the bedroom he shared with Aldona, he was as pissed as a newt. George didn't care. He just hoped he had no more bad dreams but a little later he heard furtive noises and he realised Tomas and Aldona were talking. He craned his neck in the dark to listen. The walls were paper thin. He suddenly realised that the lover's tiff they'd had over Zoya's visit had done them some good. They were obviously lovemaking, and judging by the noises they were going at it with great gusto. "Fucking greedy Baltic bastards!" he muttered, "great hosts you're turning out to be!" Tomas had chosen now to finally loosen up! George suddenly felt very lonely and unloved.

CHAPTER 13

He suffered another troubled night, unable to get away from the bad dreams. It was part sexual, part disturbing. All of it was threatening, but this one was deeper than most and the fear of being trapped hit him when he didn't emerge from it. He was somewhere else; instinctively he knew it was back home and it was something that Zoya had said during the evening which had evoked the memory.

It was in the summer garden of a house he used to live in, a house in the country. One of his daughters was playing. She couldn't have been more than three. A snake was under the stone she turned over. It seemed to stare up at her for a second, the dark, zigzag band along its slim yellow back rippling as its muscles moved. "Jill, get out of there!" he wanted to yell but his voice wouldn't work. The movements felt rusty and his throat emitted a clanking sound.

His daughter appeared to understand him, though, because she looked up, framed against the sunlight, her long hair covering her face but not entirely the laugh. "Daddy! It's only a grass snake!" she said. It was almost as if she was saying he was an idiot. He realised with a sense of shock that that's how the kids had always treated him. But she was wrong; it was an adder, and it was summer when its bite would be dangerous.

Before he could do anything the scene changed and the angel of death came to him, leathery, cruel-beaked and dominant... It raised its hammer and he cringed. He knew the pain that meant, but a thin-lipped smile on its face made him open his eyes again. He was lying naked on the bed but he couldn't rise. It was as if he was tied down but he couldn't feel any bonds and then he became aware of two other figures in the background. One was Aldona and the other Tomas. Aldona leaned over him and her breasts brushed his body. What was Tomas doing? He had a zoom lens and was taking a picture! Just as that realisation hit him he grasped Aldona roughly by the hair. It felt weird, writhing, alive, dry but smooth. He screamed; it was a knot of yellow and black snakes! He pulled away and started to scream. Tomas dropped the camera and rushed across and got hold of him. He started to shake him. He woke up to, "you are having a bad dream, my friend!"

Aldona was at the door and she was shaking her head too. "He must not be happy with himself," she added in her infuriatingly simpering way. George was gazing around wild-eyed, reliving the dream now he was awake. He looked at Aldona's hair. Stupid! It was no knot of snakes. It was just her ginger mop, a bit unrulier than usual because she'd not combed it yet and, he remembered, she had seen some action last night. The thought was like a shorting in his brain and it was accompanied by another one, more rueful: that he had been the catalyst; whatever the blockage had been, he was the juggernaut who'd removed it. Tomas held out his hand to shake his. He found the gesture a little strange. "I have to go to work now," Tomas said.

"Oh, is it that late? Well, okay, I'll see you later, won't I?"

"I don't think so," Tomas replied. "I have to fly to Norway today, on business, and I won't be back for two days. Besides our business here is done. You have your money. The phone is working again and you can ring and check if you wish."

Funny, but hadn't Tomas always said he'd run him to the airport? He wasn't going to get his triumphal moment after all when he told the jerk what a great lay his wife was. Best not to push it now, he thought. "Oh, right, Tomas, no need, I didn't mean it like that," he lied. "Well, it's been nice doing business with you, old son, but you're right, then, there's not much point in me hanging around." Except he had to of course, because Zoya had said she would see him at three that afternoon. Tomas didn't know that and, the way Zoya had put it, she didn't want anyone to know. Not even her brother or his wife. They might spoil it if they did know, so he said nothing.

It was, however, as if Tomas had read his thoughts. "There's a flight to Heathrow at eight o'clock tonight," he said, "Aldona might be able to run you to the airport."

"Or I can get a taxi," George said. "I don't want to put Aldona out." His eyes caught hers as he said it. She was still hanging around at the door looking pretty and provocative. She looked every bit the happy, contented wife. Whatever the problem had been, Tomas had come with the cure.

"You'll be all right now?" Tomas interrupted his thoughts in his concerned way. "Aldona will look after you? I trust you'll be able to spend a better day than yesterday."

George looked at Aldona. "Oh, I think I'll be okay," he replied. Tomas smiled at him sardonically. It may have been merely his gathering paranoia that made him think the younger man was no doubt satisfied with his own performance and contrasting it with George's selfish wham-bam-thank-you-ma'am apology for one. He began to walk towards the door but before he could depart, George said, "no matter what feelings you have about the Russians, it was rude to walk out before Zoya came last night. She deserved better than that, there's nothing wrong with her, she's perfectly charming." Tomas turned and looked at him, eyes like lasers staring right through him for an extraordinary amount of time, and George was, not for the first time, captivated by the blueness of those eyes, the kind of glacier blue he had seen on ski-ing trips in the Alps from the big coaches as they wound their tortuous way down the valley, following the path of those same inexorable forces of ice. His remembered that late glimpse of Zoya's eyes: how dark they were, as if deprived of all light and he wondered how hers could be so dark and her brother's so blue. He shivered when he remembered looking into those black pools in the Indigo and then remembering nothing.

He became aware that Tomas was addressing him. "All things are not as they seem, my friend. Some people are not as they seem. With Zoya and me it is an old thing. I don't wish to speak of it."

That wasn't what he'd said last night. Then it had been all about the general. "Aldona told me you're scared of her," George taunted. "Scared of your own sister!" Angrily Tomas turned on Aldona and began to berate her. George had put his foot in it. The young woman's eyes lowered as if in shame. She cast glances between the two of them beneath her long eyelashes. She made no effort to defend herself against Tomas's tirade. Her eyes on the one hand seemed to beseech him to stop, and on the other to rebuke George for his betrayal. On the one hand he was horrified; on the other he was looking at the positive. His mind was working on how he could worm his way back into her affections, capitalize on the hurt Tomas was causing her.

As soon as his host, still fuming, had stormed out, he tried it on but she pulled away from him and, almost with contempt, pushed him aside. He was surprised at the strength in the shove. Then she gave herself away. "I thought it was Zoya you fancy, judging by the way you look at her last night. You couldn't take your greedy eyes off her!"

"As if," George said, thinking I understand this, "I could look at anyone else with you around!"

"Aaaah!" she sighed, then added sorrowfully, "you are such a liar, I saw you looking at her and I saw she said something to you when she went! What was that? A promise? Did she tell you she'd see you again?"

He suddenly felt guilty. How could she have guessed that? Well, women's intuition, that's what it was. But he couldn't exactly admit it, he couldn't tell her in case it ended up spoiling the meeting "She was just saying goodbye to me, that's all," he said, "telling me she wished she'd had more time to get to know me."

"Liar,"Aldona repeated, but now she was laughing. She stood with one leg slightly forward of the other, showing her thigh, a sexy pose.

"I'm not lying!" he protested, moving closer and groping her, "come on, get into bed, it doesn't hurt anyone, I'll show you how I feel," but she continued laughing and pulled away again.

"Have your breakfast," she said, "wait, get your strength up. You will need it soon!"

Whoa! "You mean?" he asked.

"Of course." She smiled and winked again. This time she took off the robe and paraded round in bra and knickers. She patted her own ass and then went through the door.

It was as good as a promise and he knew what she had in mind - revenge on her unfeeling husband - and he was up for it. It could be his lucky day, her and Zoya at six hour intervals. He stared after her departing figure until she shut the bathroom door. Then he went into the kitchen where she had prepared cereal and fruit. He ate with relish then caught the dog looking at him. The mangy creature was still fixing him with that glare. It was positively evil! He had to get away from it and he went and lay down on his bed, waiting for Aldona to join him. Inexplicably, she'd decided to shower too. He could hear it running. You'd have thought she'd want to shower after! But who was he to complain? A nice, fresh, warm, clean body!

He must have dozed off because he didn't hear her go until the door clicked. She hadn't even popped in to see him. She'd just sneaked out of the door, telling him one thing then doing the other. Hadn't she led him on? Did he misunderstand that? Had she looked round the door, seen he was asleep and decided not to wake him? He cursed himself for falling asleep then wondered if he'd offended her - not denied strongly enough that he

wasn't truly interested in Zoya. Now she was gone.
Just like that. He shot up in sudden fear that he was
locked in again but he remembered Tomas had given
him a key after yesterday's experience. When things
began to dawn on him, in a way it was almost a relief
she was gone. It was becoming between him and his
wits. He'd forgotten, for instance, that she'd told him
Zoya was a hypnotist. Now that could explain what
happened to him but not why. Anyway, he had to keep
his eye on the ball, telephone work and check the
readies had landed. Then he could decide whether to
keep the date with Zoya. He looked at the telephone.
What he had to communicate with Marty wasn't
necessarily something he wanted overheard. Fear of
bugging meant it would be better if he went out and
rang from somewhere else. He couldn't understand how
his mobile had run down so fast. He hadn't even
bothered to bring the charger because it usually lasted a
short trip. Now he had the key he wouldn't need to take
his bags with him. He could come and go as he pleased.
He figured it was worth enquiring if there was an earlier
plane than eight tonight.

It was a warm September day when he finally stepped
outside. The fresh air revived him and he felt over his
illness at last. That weakened the instinct to catch the
first flight out of here. If he left now he'd never find out
what happened to him. The old hag cleaning the cafe
looked at him oddly as she saw his lips moving and
heard foreign sounds coming out of his mouth, but he
didn't care, he ordered a coffee, bought a phone card

and sat down. He finished the coffee double quick and walked down the sunlit street under the oak trees until he found an empty phone box, it would be just nine o'clock in England. Maybe the bank wouldn't have told them yet the money was in. He rang up and Marty was already behind his desk, his transatlantic voice made even more gravelly by a breathing disorder. He talked in staccato fashion as if he couldn't maintain a sentence for long without taking in fresh gulps of air. "You really should give up smoking!" George joshed him lightly.

"Tell me about it," Marty wheezed back. "Where've you been? It's like raising the Sleeping Beauty! What the fuck you been up to? Women, eh?"

"The women are great," George replied, "and they're hot too." He knew Marty got off vicariously on his sexploits.

"Well, I hope your brains haven't been in your dick. I just hope you've been taking care of business."

That was a bit pointed. "Course I have," George replied, conscious of the hidden menace in Marty's voice. He was tough as ship's nails, brought up in the Bronx. Nothing but nothing came before business. More than one person who'd crossed him was now weakening the foundations of a bridge. George had always been aware that their relationship thrived on their ruthless and successful common design. The signs of weakness he had recently shown could easily lead to Marty falling on him like a ravening wolf. "That's what I was ringing to tell you," he said, "you should have that half mill in now, if you check with the Bank."

"It is in," Marty replied gruffly.

"Well, there you are then!" George said excitedly, "I can come home now, the saps are zapped."

"George," Marty said huskily, "I hope for your sake you're right about this Lithuanian deal. It looks okay on paper but can you trust these people? I mean, look what's happening in Russia."

"What do you mean? Why should we need to trust them?" George asked, his heart sinking in anticipation of bad news, as if it, before his brain, knew deep down something was wrong.

"Well, what d'you mean what do I mean?" Marty replied, "That ten mill you sent over. So the mamsers have paid the upfront fee! They paid it out of our own fucking money!"

"I sent it across? What do you mean?" George's confidence returned. He knew that couldn't be right.

"Don't be an ass'ole, George," Marty replied, "you've got the bank codes, you TT'd it, remember?"

"I TT'd it. But if that had been true you could have stopped it."

"Yeah! If I'd known you'd made that transfer."

"You didn't know?"

"How the fuck would I? The bank doesn't check with me every time we send out some frigging money. It happens all the time, provided you use the right codes. Only me and you have those George!" There was menace in the rising inflections of that last statement.

"Only you and me have the codes?"

"Yeah! Quit repeating me and quit frigging me off will you! You sent an email yesterday saying how you had to do it fast, this was too good an opportunity to miss. Fantastic you called it. You said First Atlanta was going to take it."

"You must be joking?" George exploded. "I've been on my bloody back in hospital!"

"George, you sent me an email. I replied and told you, sleep on it, do it next day. You said no way Jose. I had no idea by then it was gone but you said this is the one we've been waiting for. Are you telling me that wasn't you?"

A horrible realisation was beginning to dawn on

George. "I haven't been sending any emails."

"Sure, you did and you sounded chirpy as ever, like you'd just won the lottery."

"Marty, I'll get back to you," George said.

"I don't like the sound of this, George. You know the rules, pal. It comes off of your stack!"

George suddenly contemplated wipe out. "Marty, there's an explanation. I've been in hospital."

"You will be.....when you get back."

George laughed hollowly. "Marty, you and me go back a long way! I'll get back to you, promise," Just then the phone card ran out. Normally that really bugged him. This time he couldn't have been more relieved. He rushed out of the booth and ran down the street. Passers-by looked on in astonishment as the wild-eyed figure hurtled past them.

One advantage of Vilnius is it is relatively small and compact. George didn't stop running until he reached the headquarters of Tomas's company. He burst through the door past an astonished doorman who immediately followed him into the building. George ignored the shouts from behind him and rushed up to the desk. "Argenta UAB?" he said. "I must see them immediately." The look on the receptionist's face told him she didn't speak English. "Argenta," he repeated, "biznis buro?"

"Ne!" She shook her head in the universal negative.

"Ne, what do you mean ne?"

"Ne, ne, baigesi?"

"Does anyone here speak English?" he asked.

"Laukti," she said and she got on the telephone. He fretted and fumed for what seemed an age while she spoke in her impenetrable language to a multitude of different people. A short time later, with the uniformed commissionaire still prowling about and glowering at him from across the reception hall and looking like he was a renegade from the KGB, which he probably was, another man came out of the lift and crossed to the reception desk. He spoke for a few moments with the receptionist, both of them looking from time to time in his direction, then the man detached himself from the desk over which he had draped his long body and crossed the marble floor towards George. "Can I help you?" he said in a heavy accent.

"Oh thank God you speak English," George said. "I need to find Mr. Tomas Piechnik who works for a company called UAB Argenta. These are their offices aren't they?" he said looking wildly around. "I came here just two days ago. We had a meeting here.

Upstairs. I think it was the twentieth floor." He crossed over to the lift. "Yes, the twentieth," he confirmed.

"There are many different companies in this building," the man said. "Wait there a moment, I will make some enquiries." George sagged into one of the seats in the reception hall. He was already exhausted and it was still morning. The man spoke to the receptionist, who rang someone, then they spoke again. George looked up as once again he crossed over to him. "I'm sorry," he said, "I was wrong, there is a such a company."

"Good," George said, feeling a huge sense of relief.

"Or I should say was …? They moved out. Their lease was up yesterday. They took it for six months only."

Six months! George groaned. That was about the length of time since Tomas's call to him in London. Which of his operatives had seen him first and recommended this deal for consideration? He couldn't remember but he would and when he did he'd have his guts for garters. He tried to keep his cool. "Do you know where they've gone?" The man shouted what he assumed was the same question to the receptionist. She made another call, came off the phone, shook her head, and then said something to the man, who repeated to George, "apparently before they quit the building they left a letter to be collected by someone called Georgi."

"That'll be me," he replied, his heart sinking. All he

needed now was the business equivalent of a Dear John. A little later a courier exited the lift. He gave the letter to the man who looked at it, then he was about to hand it to George but he suddenly thought better of it. George groaned as he took out his passport for identification purposes. The man scanned it and then the name on the envelope and, satisfied they related to the same person, he handed it over. George took it, unable to disguise his trembling hand. As he read the contents, the colour drained from his face. The man looked at him with an expression of concern. George looked back at him. There was nothing he could say. He could try and hold them responsible because they were in the same building but he knew that would get short shrift in the UK, let alone here. When he thought about it he couldn't even be sure this bloke wasn't in on it. Tomas might even now be watching him on closed circuit TV pissing himself laughing while his sidekick gave George the bum's rush! That was exactly how it felt. "Sorry," the man said, "we can't help more."

Discretion getting the better part of valour, because, in fact, he wanted to lambast the guy, curse him and his fucking building and most of all his fucking pathetic little nation full of thieves and mountebanks, "thanks," George replied glumly, and he retraced his steps to the door. He went into the first bar he could find, ordered a pint of the local brew and sat down to re-read the letter in case he'd missed something which might give him a sign of hope.

"Dear Georgi," it read, *"so sorry to have played a trick on you. It was necessary because you were going to do the dirty on us. Oh yes, we know that. We looked at your portfolio the night you got drunk. We returned it intact did we not? It was useful you retained the bank codes and we are grateful to you. Whatever else is said it was very good doing business with you. We enjoyed it very much. We hope it wasn't all bad for you as well. Now, I suppose you'll be thinking of making all sorts of dire threats. Oh yes, we checked you out. We talked to a lot of companies you did so-called business with (but they call it getting ripped off) and we kept a copy of your dossier to show to your Government in case you try any bully-boy stuff. It is very hard to make money here. Much easier where you come from. Easy come, easy go, that is your saying isn't it? I too found this very easy come but it will not be easy go. You can congratulate yourself you have helped a lot of needy people. Goodbye for now. I hope we don't meet again because if we do I may have to deal with you in a way I would not like. I hope your partners go easy on you. Aldona says, bye big boy".* It was signed simply, *Tomas.*

George put the letter down and sipped morosely at his pint. It looked like there was no way back on this one. He had to think quickly, though, keep his cool. He needed to find Tomas. Maybe he could convince him of the danger he'd put him in. He'd got to know the Lithuanian quite well. He wasn't a bad lad. He'd seen the main chance and played George for a mug, all credit to him, he'd really pulled that off well, but George had a feeling about him, he didn't seem like a crook. If the bank had been genuine, did that mean the deal would have gone ahead, Tomas wouldn't have pulled this scam? He figured that might have been the case and if that was true then, even now, he could salvage something by persuading him to make the bank's investment a true one. At least that way he could fob his partners off for another six months, perhaps a year, and who knows, the deal might work? It was that last but one line, where Tomas was saying he hoped George's partners would go easy on him. Maybe he didn't realise how brutal they would be. If he understood that, perhaps he'd compromise.

Filled with renewed hope, he still had the problem of getting in touch with Tomas. It was a long shot but Zoya had said she would be at the flat this afternoon. Maybe she meant it. As a betting man, he'd have given no odds on her turning up but stranger things have happened. This place was off the wall! And it wasn't as if he had a lot in the way of alternatives. In fact, Zoya turning up at the flat was the only chance he had to make contact again. He had the uneasy feeling that fate had corralled him into a corner.

CHAPTER 14

Shell-shocked by the events of the past few days and having no choice but to kill some time before the three o' clock appointment, George walked on to the next bar. He didn't normally drink at this time of day but he needed another to calm his nerves because he couldn't get one thought out of his head: how could a person he liked to think of as a twat take him for a ride like that? He had mixed it with some of the sharpest dealers on the planet and prided himself that he saw the sting coming long before you heard the wasp. He knew exactly how it worked. Successful con-men always had excellent credentials, a great idea, a solid looking foundation. They were credible people, hard-working, the exact opposite of the type you'd expect.

There was nothing remotely fancy about Tomas or his scam: earnest, youthful, even slightly effeminate young lad, patriotic to a fault, desperate to do something for the new Republic of Lithuania, and to make a name for himself in the process, convinces tertiary London merchant bankers to back a project which can't lose, an industrial project carried out already in the developed world so the market already exists. The angle for the profit comes from the fact that there is a workforce trained to near western standards, a safe infrastructure now they're away from the Soviets, a real hunger to learn and progress and, most important of all, 10 years of guaranteed cheap labour while the slack is reined in. A real prospect for a successful investment.

Just the way any decent sting would be set up. But George had fallen for it. In fact the only reason George had scammed it rather than run with it was Tomas's own insistence on the deal being long term with only limited dividends in the early days. The deal didn't fit the profile of the usual sub-prime western investment model because it couldn't guarantee return of capital quickly enough. Tomas and his colleagues had no track record so they had been forced to go to one of the fringe investment funds. George's bank came highly recommended. Ha! That was rich! They were targeted! The stinger was set up to be stung!

It was difficult but he was coming to terms with it. Tomas had been a con man all along. As George sipped his beer he was thinking hard. The operation had gone like clockwork. Even Aldona giving him one yesterday morning was intended to up the feel-good factor! It made him feel he was in control, relaxed him when he was getting jittery, then she'd buggered off, pretending to be satisfied out of her brains, and she'd locked him in. The telephone wasn't working. If he'd made the phone call to Marty yesterday he could have stopped that payment going through and Tomas had known that from the day before because of the 24 hour delay. That's why he'd insisted on George staying at their flat. No, hold on, it was the Scouser who suggested that. Oh no, the thought that he was in on it too was just too awful to conjure with. He was a doctor for fuck's sake! What was his reason for doing that? Yeah but he was a colleague of hers, wasn't he? Of Zoya's. They probably all danced to her spell. And what of her, the mystery woman this all started with? She must be in it up to her neck! She set him up, met him in the bar and then, well ...heaven only knew what she did to him. Talk about wham, bam, thank you ma'am, this woman reinvented bordello rules! They'd stop at nothing, this bunch.

That's why they all came round yesterday evening, to cover for Tomas's absence while he went and sorted the bank, cloned his email address and sent mails off in his name to keep everyone at the other end happy. That way they maintained that disorientating effect they'd had on him, kept him off balance. He could see it all now: Zoya had hypnotised him; they'd got his briefcase and seen his notes, realised he was going to scam them and they'd photocopied the bank codes and returned them. They'd got his email address, run his phone power down, not even nicked his phone, not done anything clumsy like that. They'd just put everything back the way it was and pretended nothing untoward had happened. It had all been natural. He shook his head. "What a mug!" he said.

A pale skinned man with short greasy hair parted in three places from the crown to the forehead detached himself from a stool near the bar and sidled over to him. "You American?" he asked in a thick Russian accent.

George looked at the man. He seemed to have a sneering attitude. "No," he replied curtly hoping that would make him go away.

The man persisted. "Eengleesh?" he enquired. Irritated now George nonetheless nodded. He just wanted to be left alone with his troubles, wondering what sort of reception committee Marty would have planned for him when he got home. Jen would know what to do. If only he hadn't burnt his boats there. He'd left himself isolated, no one to turn to. He who had always been able to take care of any problem! Then he remembered his last nightmare. His daughter! But no, it was an adder and he had been there. He could make the nightmare right in retrospect. He had saved her. He'd hit the snake first time with a brick, an unerring shot, and it had scuttled off while Jill cried because she didn't want him to hurt the creature! Jesus, when he thought about the closeness of that it nearly brought him to tears. And now she just kept the money and sent back the birthday cards all manked up! What had he done to make them feel that way about him? Out of the corner of his eye, he saw the man sit down next to him. Oh no, he thought, there's one bar in Vilnius with a nutter and I walk right into it. "You wanna see Vilnius?" the man said. "I take you round. I got taxi."

George waved his hands in a gesture of dismissal. "No," he said, "no way," and his troubles came to the surface as he added bitterly, "no way do I want to see any more of this poxy city or its thieving inhabitants!"

He could tell immediately he'd done the wrong thing. The man looked offended. "You Eeengleesh you treat us like third world - "

" - Sorry, sorry," George said, holding up his hands now in a gesture of surrender, "I've had a hard couple of days, I'm sorry, I just let myself get carried away."

He tried to explain that he'd spent some time in hospital in Vilnius, exaggerating the time spent and the ailment, so as to mollify the Lithuanian but it just seemed to incense him more. "You been getting treatment at one of our hospital, you pay for it, eh? I been waiting ages to get treatment. You seen this, you seen this!" George was astonished as the man dropped his trousers in the middle of the bar and stuck his white belly in his face. He looked around wildly but no one gave it a second glance. The Lithuanian insisted aggressively on George seeing his scar and how it was still red and weeping slightly. "This happen to me in accident," the man went on, "I have to wait years for treatment and you, you bastard, you come here, get pissed out of your brain and they take you into hospital and give you good treatment so you can call them sheet after."

The Lithuanian was raving on like a lunatic. George thought he wasn't going to get rid of him so he stuffed his hand in his pocket and took out some notes. "Sorry pal," he said, "I didn't mean to give the impression I was ungrateful. Your doctors and nurses are great, your country's great." He stuffed the notes in the man's hand.

The Lithuanian stood up, stared at George with a mad look in his eyes and flung the notes at him. "You think you can screw me," he screamed, "I kill you, you Eeengleesh bastard!" The proprietor of the bar, a sallow skinned man, had crept up surreptitiously behind the lunatic just as George was beginning to feel truly threatened. The barman grabbed the man's arms and held them tight to his side in a bear hug. Soothingly he spoke to him. There was something incredibly gentle about it, as if he knew the man well and this behaviour was nothing strange. He looked at George and said, "The KGB did this to him. It okay."

George looked back at the barman, who nodded to him, indicating with a sideways shift of his head the direction of the door. George needed no further persuasion. He started to shovel up the money but the barman now released the quiescent lunatic and used his left hand to restrain George's exertions. George looked up at him and the man shook his head. He started to protest and the barman said, "it's for the house, for the damage!"

"What damage?" George exclaimed looking about him. The barman kicked over a stool. He smiled at George a condescending sort of smile. "That damage. Eeengleesh hooligan!"

George said, "do you realise I know your Police Chief, I know your Interior Minister?"

"Oh that's nice, so they pay for the damage? How about you collect it from them, huh?" the barman replied. A number of other customers were looking at the proceedings with interest and he was well outnumbered. Besides the barman looked pretty handy. "Quick, before it cost more," he added with a sinister chuckle.

George was beaten. He'd never experienced a place quite like this. "Baltic fucking bastards!" he snarled.

"Yeah, yeah," the barman grinned and he made a limp gesture with his hand. George headed for the door. He heard ripples of laughter behind him and saw the whole bar had joined in. Angrily, through the window, he gave them a V sign but the laughter only increased, augmented by jeers and catcalls.

Still needing a safe haven he found the most select restaurant he could and went in. A waiter showed him to a table where he ordered a steak and a bottle of red wine. He sat there glumly, drinking away, wishing the time would just pass by so he could go back to the apartment, either sort out the problem or, if there was no one there, cut his losses and get out of here. The food arrived. He sipped thoughtfully at his wine as he ate. Funny how he'd woken up this morning without a care in the world. Zoya had told him she'd see him this afternoon, another con no doubt just to keep him on the hop, and then he'd thought he was on the verge of slipping Aldona one as she paraded round the kitchen like a little slut, angry with her husband for his tirade of abuse. Only she'd walked out, by which time no doubt Tomas had got far away from any possible retribution. Jesus, when he thought about it, he had to hand it to them. And he'd accused this bunch of being amateurs! They'd run it like clockwork. But what about the doctors? Why did they get involved?

And then he remembered what they'd been celebrating at the party last night. His frame slumped further into his chair as he realised that the story of the frigging general, whose son they'd saved only for him to die later fighting in Chechnya, was probably another smokescreen. What had they called that new wing? St. George's! Oh! He slammed his knife down with a bang that made all the diners turn round simultaneously. "Fucking hell," he shouted, oblivious to them all, "I've donated the hospital a new sodding children's wing! You bitch! You absolute bitch! That's out of order, that is!" He was of course referring now to the beautiful Zoya. It somehow made it worse that, in this speculation, she was an altruistic con artist. One of the waiters detached himself from the back wall and began to move across towards him. "The cheeky bloody cow! Is that taking the piss or what?" The waiter was standing over him now. "Aldona told me," he told the man, "she said her speciality was hypnosis, they bloody hypnotised me and told me to talk to Marty and frigging

214

send that money over here. Like a bunch of dipsticks we all fell for it. Talk about the three card trick!"

"I'm sorry, sir," the waiter was saying, "you'll have to leave, you're disturbing the other guests," and gently he started to ease George out of the chair.

"Don't manhandle me," George said, pulling himself away violently and moving his chair back with a screech. "Just get me the bloody bill!" The wine had taken hold of him and he staggered uneasily to the counter to pay as the waiter followed, looking concerned about what he would do next. Most of the diners were looking at him open-mouthed, some were shaking their heads in disgust. "Don't you bleeding well shake your heads at me!" he yelled, pointing round the room accusingly, "I can buy and sell yous lot ten times over!"

The waiter had been joined by a number of his colleagues and, although they didn't touch George, their combined presence moved him towards the cashier who was furiously printing out his bill. The machine seemed to go on interminably. "What the hell's happening?" George shouted at her, "Don't tell me I'm paying for every other bugger in the restaurant! It's just one bill you know. Just me."

The woman handed him the bill and he scrutinised it quickly. He squinted at it and couldn't read it in the poor light inside the restaurant. He felt in his breast pocket and as his hand closed over them an awful thought occurred to him. He reached inside his pocket further and his already slack jaw fell further. Oh no, he thought again, his wallet had gone, all his credit cards. It must have been the madman at the pub whilst his attention was caught by his crazy ravings. He'd been set up again! Now, how did he get out of this? "Can't read the bill," he explained, thinking on his feet, "forgot my glasses!"

"What?" the head waiter said.

"Spectacles!" George said, and he made round binocular shapes next to his eyes. The head waiter took a moment to realise what he meant and then he clapped his hands and called to a colleague. Everyone turned away from him momentarily and George was gone. He did a runner, out into the street before they'd even noticed he was no longer there, and then he heard the shouts behind as they followed him.

He ran until his lungs were bursting and then he came to a church. It was a Catholic church. He rushed inside, scampered up the aisle in front of the large figure of Christ and knelt down perspiring in a pew near the altar. He was pretending to pray, for the benefit of the disparate groups of people who were in there, but in truth he was keeping an eye on the door. He stiffened suddenly. The posse had arrived. A group of men in black tie congregated in the doorway, uneasy at disturbing the peace of the church, then, padding silently and determinedly along the flagged aisles, they began a methodical sweep of the pews. George ducked down, his heart pounding. All he needed now was to be arrested by the Stasi or whatever they called the feds here. He was desperate to get on a flight home, but it looked as if he was going to be battered to death by a bunch of revengeful Baltic waiters. He'd had the KGB hospital; it looked like the gulag next. He heard footsteps approaching and sweated more profusely. What to do? Fight? Run for it? Try and talk his way out of it? It was no good, the game was up, the shadow was almost over him now. Cowering, trembling fearfully, he glanced up. Towering over him was the figure of a Catholic priest. He spoke to George in Lithuanian. George shook his head. All he could do was croak, "I'm British."

"Ah!" the priest said, and then he addressed him in English. "It is all right, they have gone now, I have sent them away."

"Thank you father, oh thank you." George just managed to restrain himself from clinging on to the priest's cassock. He drew himself up, still looking round warily, when the priest took his arm and said, "come on, I will show you another way out, in case they are outside." George nodded gratefully and followed the priest through a door behind the altar. "Will you have coffee?" the priest asked him. "You look as if you need something." George thanked him. He took the proffered cup, sat down on the wooden bench and drank the warm liquid greedily. It wasn't that he was thirsty, it was the comfort of the warmth. The priest sat down next to him. "Perhaps I can help you with your problem? Would you like to tell me why those men were chasing you?"

Grateful for the opportunity to talk to someone, he blurted out the story from when he'd gone in the bar and been accosted by the nutter, how he didn't realise his wallet had been stolen until he had to pay the bill in the restaurant. The priest listened to him sympathetically but when he'd finished, said, "Yes, that was unfortunate, but you are not telling me everything, you would not have run away like that if this was all there was to it. You look like a respectable businessman. The restaurant owner would have understood your plight and come to some arrangement."

George realised he was right and embarked on the convoluted tale of what had happened to him since he'd arrived in Lithuania. He was careful only to tell the priest the things which cast him in a good if unlucky light. He told him nothing which would detract from the impression that he was a victim. The priest listened gently to his tale of woe and again, when he had finished, he nodded his head sagaciously, but then he replied, "But you are still not telling the whole truth, are you? You are hiding something, perhaps even from yourself. Sometimes the tragedies we suffer tell us more about ourselves and our own circumstances than they do about the circumstances of the apparent oppressor."

George looked at him and his lip curled. "Are you saying I've brought all this on myself?" he asked contemptuously. Just what he needed, an unctuous dose of homespun philosophy.

The priest nodded. "I am saying," he replied, "that until you come to terms with why these things happened to you, you will not be able to resolve them. Even worse, you will not be safe."

"What do you mean, I'll not be safe?"

"Just that. Your troubles may not have ended yet."

"Explain yourself," George said, "how would you know?" But the priest, who had an incredibly strong arm and lithe, powerful frame, was impelling him with a grip like iron towards the back door. He opened it and cast George out, as if he were an evil spirit. "Oh, well, that's your Christian charity for you, isn't it?" George yelled from outside, then he remembered he was still on the run so he took a furtive look round and, satisfied it was all clear, hared off down the back street until he was sure he'd lost all trace of his pursuers.

When he stopped running he discovered he was down on the bank of the river Neris in the lee of the Zirmunai Bridge near where he'd first been stopped by the soldier after his arrival and he sat down on a bench. That encounter seemed a century ago! He was lost in Vilnius. He had no money. He didn't dare ask anyone for help in case they ripped him off too. His head sank on to his hands. He'd never experienced such a catalogue of disasters. Nothing had gone right since he'd walked out on his wife for that Aussie bird. She'd been all right at first but then she'd started to get demanding, like they all did. They all fed off him. Parasites! He kept the lot in the style to which they'd become accustomed (only because of him) and now they expected no less of him. So when his efforts didn't quite match up to their expectations, when he didn't quite deliver what they wanted, they all acted as if he'd betrayed them, as if he was the biggest bastard in the world. Then all they wanted was a chunk out of his hide! He had to give this one a property, let that one keep the Roller – he'd only known her a short time but because he'd put it in her name to dodge the taxman he'd had to write it off! They all frigging blackmailed him, every confidence he'd given them was rammed back in his face. The only one who hadn't let him down was Jen. But she was a real lady, way above that kind of thing. Her father hadn't wanted her to marry him but he'd set his cap at her because her old man was wealthy and any likely lad can do with a hand up. It was handy he'd got her pregnant. That way everyone had to just bite the bullet. But George had to admit her old man had had a point. He'd caused her nothing but grief and look at him now: fate was having a right go back. It was his darkest hour. Suddenly, possibly for the first time ever, he felt small, afraid, vulnerable, perhaps even a little bit human.

Watching the grey river flow by, he saw a white duck. It swam around in the water, dipping its head beneath the surface from time to time in search of food. Each time it came up it shook its feathers. Suddenly, out of the corner of his eye, George saw a large bird swoop. It was a hawk, probably a kestrel. There was something familiar about it, then he remembered the dream. "The angel of death!" he exclaimed. The hawk went straight for the duck in a controlled stoop. George was suddenly frightened. He *was* the duck. He reached down and picked up a stone. He flung it at the water. The duck took off. The hawk cried as it missed its stoop but it didn't give up. It quickly regained height and repeated the manoeuvre, only this time with greater success, taking the duck out in flight, hitting it behind the neck with sledgehammer force and downing it on to the bank where its voracious beak ripped out the poor beast's entrails. George shook himself; his heart pounded; he was wet with shock and fear; then he looked up towards the bridge. A figure was staring at him. He squinted into the weak sunlight. His heart skipped a beat.

The more he looked the surer he felt it was Tomas. He stood up and started to walk towards the distant figure. It stayed still. George shouted. There was no response. He began to run up the steps and, for the first time, the figure detached itself and disappeared. George yelled at the top of his voice. The passer by coming down the steps stared. George ran to the top of the steps but he couldn't see Tomas. Running towards the cobbled square, he reached the corner and saw the figure with its back to him. It disappeared round the next corner. Shouting again, he followed just in time to see it turn the next corner. George usually kept himself pretty fit, he had his own gym in the house and he liked to pump iron with his personal trainer, but he had to admit, what with his separation and its effect on his routine and the way things had turned out here, he wasn't in the best of condition. The sweat was beginning to stand out on his brow and he was panting by the time he reached the end of the maze of cobbled streets.

If it was Tomas - and why should anyone else run away from him? - He had disappeared but not without bringing George home. There in front of him was the block of flats in which Tomas and Aldona lived. He breathed out gratefully. That at least gave him the chance of escape. He had money and some more credit cards in his case, and he had air tickets. Worst ways he could get out of this god-forsaken place and put the whole nightmare behind him. There might well be another battle to face with Marty and his other partners, and he might end up on his toes yet again, but he was still in there fighting. He'd survived the worst they could throw at him here.

He went through the revolving door into the block. Just to compound everything else the lift had packed up again. He swore as he walked up to the tenth floor. By the time he reached it his heart was pumping. The alcohol he'd consumed didn't help. He mopped his brow and breathed out heavily as he tried the key. He'd had a half idea it wouldn't work but it turned and the door opened. He didn't expect anyone to be there when he got back. He knew they'd have done a moonlight because he would have in their shoes but he didn't know whether to laugh or cry. On the one hand he would have liked to have a go at that pansy Tomas for making such a cherry of him. On the other, if he'd come here and found them mob-handed he'd have been shit-scared. He looked at his watch. It was three o'clock. Funny, bit of a coincidence that, he'd arrived back at the time Zoya had said she would come and see him. But that was all bullshit. He'd fallen for that one too. He felt like the Red Indians must have when someone took a photograph of them without their permission. Zoya had stolen his soul. He breathed a sigh of relief as soon as he opened his case. His credit cards were still there. So who needed a soul these days? It was all about travelling light. The soul's a very heavy thing to carry.

CHAPTER 15

It was a scratching noise. He hadn't noticed it at first but it became apparent after a few seconds and it made him drop his bag and stand there stock still. He craned his head, listening, thinking he'd imagined the sound. Why was everything always so silent in this building, was it peopled with ghosts? Then it came again. Someone was trying a key in the lock. There was a bang on the door. The noise reverberated through the apartment. His scalp prickled. He could hear the key turning and it was as if it was happening in slow motion, like in one of those horror movies. He'd half expected it but when it did happen the expectation made it all the more shocking.

The way things had happened, it seemed his return was almost predestined. All his life was like coming back here – doing things he knew instinctively were wrong. Everyone knew the world was mad; everyone knew things were wrong; everyone wanted to get off the rollercoaster; everyone gritted his teeth waiting for it to finally derail; but, like a gambler betting his life on the next chamber being empty, everyone went for the next shot. George eased his way to the bedroom door and peered through the crack into the corridor, just as the front door opened.

Tomas! It was Tomas. He was momentarily disappointed. He had hoped for Zoya. But Tomas was a consolation prize. Maybe he could force him to put things right. He recalled how he'd gone to his business premises to plead with him. Stepping back behind the door, George waited for him to come through. Several scenarios flashed through his mind simultaneously. To challenge him or to humour him? What was he trying to achieve here? Was it achievable more by threat than by inducement? He'd know soon enough. Tomas had completed his grand tour, no doubt checking he'd left no clue behind, and now he was approaching the kitchen. George sprang out as he entered. He went straight for the younger man, bowling him over on to the concrete floor. Standing over him, arms at his sides like a gorilla, he said, "Tomas, me old mucker! How are you?" That's how confident he felt. One to one with the wimp, no problem! The best way of getting his attention? Knock him on his ass!

Tomas sat up on the floor and moved back slightly so he could look George in the eye. "Georgi," he said, "you're still here?" It wasn't surprise; it was a question.

"Large as life," George replied. "As if I could possibly leave without seeing yous. Yous and me need to have a bit of a chat, sunshine."

"Oh no, I don't think so," Tomas responded, and, demonstrating unsuspected agility, he jumped to his feet without using his arms, almost like one of those

Cossack dancers you saw at the circus. George immediately went into a half-crouch and Tomas laughed. "What's wrong, Georgi? I'm not going to hurt you!"

"Nowt's the matter," George replied with a snarl, "but yous and me have unfinished business."

"On the contrary," Tomas said in his clipped English, "our business is actually totally at an end." He made a sideways chopping motion with both hands, signifying the finality. "Finito! Kaputt! Over! You get my drift?"

"No it's not, not until I get my money back it ain't. Until then I'll say when it's over."

Tomas held out his hands. "Georgi, whatever I do, I cannot restore to you what you consider to be rightfully yours. You know all about overheads, don't you? It is very important to your bank not to incur too many or to ensure that if they do then they are paid from some source other than the bank's own resources. It is no different here. The overheads of an operation like this are immense and they have to be accounted for from somewhere. There are bills to pay, people to look after, commitment fees to meet." He nodded at George. "You understand those, don't you? You are a businessman so you will appreciate the effort that has gone into this project? I cannot short-change these people. Some of them would not be forgiving. Some of them are mob-connected. Do you understand what I mean by that?"

"Mob? Mob? You think you know the mob? I can show you mob. When my guys get hold of you, you will wish you were dead! There will be no mercy, no quarter. Your only chance is to make a deal with me."

Tomas regarded this with barely controlled mirth. "Georgi," he said, "what you perhaps don't appreciate is that there are a lot of people in this country who are used to dealing with trouble. A lot of very handy lads who have nothing to do now there is no more national service in the Soviet army. Yes, you have the mob and I am sure it is a very cruel, ruthless mob. But here, you see, we have nothing. The people here are just trying to survive so we have a mob too. It is not a fat cat mob, it is a very lean and sinewy mob; it is not an eat all you can for five Great British pounds mob, it is a very hungry eat what you can kill mob. You have probably not thought about it but I am sure you will agree that it doesn't go to your country and interfere with your mob there and, conversely, it doesn't much like it when the mob from over there tries to muscle in on the meagre resources of the mob over here. Georgi, let me tell you about ruthless. You have heard of the S.S, yes? The Schutzstaffel? The Nazi German Secret Police? Yes? Is that ruthless enough for you? The most ruthless regiment the S.S ever had, the Einsatzgruppe, was raised in Lithuania. You see, we do this very well. This is a very small country but people disappear easily here and no one cares. You catch my drift? The forests are very deep and full of swamps. They will look here and they will look there and then the police chief will just round up the usual suspects. They won't be anyone of any consequence. Nothing will happen. Time will tick away. People will move on."

George knew he should be heeding this. Tomas was trying to tell him to go home and forget about it but he just couldn't. Simple as that. He didn't come from a race of quitters. The gurgle started in his abdomen, moved up to his chest and came out of his throat as a roar. Whatever ideas of diplomacy he had once espoused, whatever conscience of Tomas's he had hoped to appeal to, they went to the wind as his hatred surfaced. He hurled himself at Tomas, knocking him back to the kitchen bench. They circled each other. George tried to goad him. "Your wife's a good little screw," he taunted. "Did she tell you how she mounted me? She couldn't get enough, the little tart. That's all you people are good for, pretty boy."

With a bloodcurdling shout he launched himself again at the slighter man and, head down, charging like a bull, he took him in the stomach and forced him back. What sounded like laughter emerged from Tomas's throat and it only served to enrage George further. The two wrestled round the kitchen, banging into the table, the cupboards, the sink, until George was black and blue. Tomas, with surprising strength, imprisoned the older man's arms, making it impossible for him to punch for the stomach. George's head was buried into Tomas's chest. It seemed soft and insubstantial, he didn't know where the younger man's strength came from. The two separated momentarily. George was blowing hard; Tomas wasn't even sweating. He still had a grin on his face and he was making the moves now, up on his toes, mocking George: "float like a butterfly, sting like a bee!" he was saying with his mocking, accented, perfect English.

Still feeling his advantage in power would pay, George charged again, head down, going for the grapple. This time Tomas knew what to expect. His foot snaked out like lightning, catching George under the chin. George's head snapped back and he almost turned a full back somersault. Shocked, he staggered to his feet but his legs weren't quite there and Tomas took him full in the chest with a double fronted drop kick, his voice high-pitched, Bruce Lee style, in triumph. George felt as if his whole ribcage had caved in; it was like being stabbed with twin daggers. He tried to keep his feet but he went over backwards. He hit the concrete floor with a crack that made him think his back was broken. He struggled to get up but he couldn't. All was dark in front of him as if he had taken one in the eye which had closed off his vision.

Tomas, though, seemed to fall into his hands. Over confident, he leaned too close and George caught his adversary in a bear hug. Strangely, he made no effort to pull clear. "Got you!" George grimaced, his arms encircling the younger man's ribcage. His eyesight started to return in a blur in which Tomas appeared smiling. George was crushing him but the idiot was smiling! Too late he looked to his left and saw the hypodermic sticking out of his shoulder. Tomas's thumb pressed inwards and the green fluid disappeared from the phial. "What the fuck!" George muttered and he looked back at those dark eyes gazing down at him. *Dark eyes!* Tomas's were the brightest blue George had ever seen, like alpine glaciers. His head began to fill with mist and his arms went numb. As he went into the prone, crucifix position Tomas disentangled himself and strutted round his prostrate victim. The last image he saw in his mind's eye was his own mouth gaping. Tomas was very much a woman.

CHAPTER 16

It was that fucking angel again, giving him grief with the hammer. He also had a throbbing pain in his arms. He was lying in warm water and his wrists were tied behind his head. He could feel every aching rib. Then his memory came back. Was this meant to be some kind of bizarre joke? Only this time he wasn't in his hotel room but in the bathroom at Tomas's apartment. He became aware of someone in the other room. "Tomas?" he croaked, his mouth nearly filling with water as he moved and caused a tidal wave.

The door creaked as it opened fully. It wasn't Tomas but it was Zoya. Despite the sinking feeling in the pit of his stomach he was beginning to have his suspicions about this, that it might not be quite as bad as it looked. She hadn't killed him; she could have killed him; she hadn't. It gave him hope. He'd met people who lived their lives by the principle that humanity was worthless, nothing more than a pile of genes, it didn't matter whether you heaped more misery on the paupers of the world, or granted even more largesse to those who already had it coming out of their ears. In other words it all meant nothing. There was just you against everyone else. It's like locusts. Everyone wonders why they swarm in their millions across hundreds of miles and cause such devastation, devouring everything in their sight. There's an even more horrible secret behind it than the horrible sight of these creatures in themselves. They are desperate for protein and the nearest protein is the fellow creature in front. They are cannibals and the only way they can stop themselves being eaten is to swarm onwards and devour what is in their path. They can't show weakness; if they do they will be dead and the swarm's next meal. The point was, if these people had been like that, he would be dead now. So maybe the race was not yet run, maybe there was still all to play for, and that is, after all, how he had lived his life up to now.

"Ah, Georgi, you are awake," Zoya said. She was actually dressed in a bathrobe and she had been doing her nails because she kept them away from the cloth and he could see the blueness. She came now and sat on the edge of the bath as if the two of them were intimate friends, and perhaps they were, in the strange comradeship of cruelty. "I am so pleased, I thought I'd injected a little too much." She shook her head regretfully.

George smiled inwardly. She was proving his thesis out of her own mouth. He decided to be bold. His head hurt terribly but he managed: "why don't you stop playing this game and let me out of here?"

"Oh, but Georgi, you may become violent again," she replied. "You have such a propensity for bullying." Funny. Jen had said something similar. He didn't have that perception of himself but that was the least of his problems at the moment. He had to talk his way out of this predicament first. He had an idea how to do it; he'd seen enough criminal profiling programmes on the telly and at the movies. The secret was to keep her talking, build a relationship with her, but he had to appreciate also that he was dealing with someone unbalanced, a psychopath in fact, someone whose moods could swing in a moment. "No way," he said, "you've got the better of me, girl, I know when I'm beat. I'm not a glutton for punishment. Tell you what, you just let me go, I'll walk away and you'll never hear from me again." Yes, it was him saying this, he thought. A few moments ago all he had wanted was to recover the bank's money but now he couldn't care less. It just wasn't important any more. He wanted to save his hide. It seemed there were more important things than money but you didn't realise it until you right up against the eight ball.

"Oh, how nice it would be to release you! And so easy! If only I could trust you Georgi," she replied, laughing now, a curiously pleasant feminine chime, as if she wasn't a sadist at all. "But, you see, we both know I can't trust you. You'll go and complain to the Police and all those authorities you are so well in with -"

" - No, I won't, I promise, I'm out of here, you've got it wrong, I don't want any more of this, I promise, you let me go and I'll just take off out of here." As if to emphasise his promise he made aeroplane droning noises, wishing he could do the wings but it was a bit difficult with his hands tied. His elbows flapped helplessly by his sides. In his mind's eye they looked more like a frustrated chicken's than an aeroplane's. He unbalanced himself and his head was suddenly submerged. He was choking.

When he came back up spluttering, she was talking smoothly. "Oh, but I know you'll leave here straight away, but then, as soon as no one is watching you any more, you'll go to your Foreign Office and tell terrible tales all about the nasty bandits who stole your money and kidnapped you and tied you up and immersed you in water. Twice. And before you know it all those clever policemen over where you come from will be doing those E-fits and the not so clever policemen over here will be forced to make it look like they are interested. The temperature will get hotter for everyone. This is kidnapping, isn't it, Georgi? Abduction? Isn't that what they call it? Before you know it Interpol gets involved and then the police over here will come after us because we can't have foreign nationals treated like that in our splendid country and our beautiful, peaceful capital city. What! Tied up like wild animals! What is the world coming to? Can you see how parliament expressing its disapproval?" Her eyes opened startlingly wide. They were stunning in their dark depths. "It will be like the Saugumas all over again."

"The what?"

"I am talking about the Lithuanian Nazi Police of the

wartime, collaborative, provisional government."

"Hey, I wouldn't know anything about that, pet!" He was trying his best to sound light-hearted. "But no way would I do any of those things you said. I would just keep mum. I know when to shut it, I do."

"No? You wouldn't do any of those things?" Her eyebrows arched into an interrogatory mark?

"I swear it, kid."

"Ah dear, there you go again, as if your word is worth anything? Didn't we have your word that you would deal with us fairly?"

"Well, what are you going to do with me then?" George asked suspiciously. He was getting irritated by the game now. It was becoming worrying unreal. "What did you do with me last time? Hypnosis?"

"What a clever guess! But the Indigo was far too crowded for conventional hypnosis, so I had to use artificial aids. In your country you will know them as benzodiazepines or GHB but here we have some unusual compounds which are far more sophisticated. It is one thing we have to thank the KGB for. They were quite the experts at all sorts of things. Pain, of course, that was their speciality, but there are far more subtle getting information out of people without them even knowing they are giving it."

The penny dropped with George. "So you drugged me but so I could still do things, tell you things?" he asked suspiciously. He was thinking he'd used Rohypnol on women for a bit of a lark and he remembered it kind of had that effect. They just performed naturally but didn't actually know they were doing it. He'd never expected it to be turned on him. He was uneasy with the thought. He didn't want Zoya to learn that.

"It was so easy too. You are a very good subject, Georgi." She added that as if half scolding him. "Unfortunately on this latest occasion, when we met here, you were behaving a little too wildly, you were thoroughly unreasonable! I had to quench your ardour and then put you in these awful bonds afterwards! The body temperature drops very quickly in the first hour so it is necessary to create a warm environment. The bath is ideal." She made it sound as if there had been no other choice.

"Unreasonable? You're kidding me aren't you?" He tried to make it sound humorous. "You waltz off with all my cash, put my life in danger. All right, you might think it's a pretty worthless life but it's the only one I've got!"

"Oh Georgi, you are a natural funny man! You should be on the stage!"

"You start off as a bloke then you change into a bird

and you still beat seven tons of shit out of me! You drug me, tie me up and shove me in the bath. Twice! And I just happen to point out that's no way to treat a lover, baby? Unreasonable or what?"

She was laughing now. "You are sometimes so witty Georgi, you have missed your vocation!"

"And you, are you really a doctor?" he asked in a puzzled voice.

"Oh yes," she replied, "I am the night doctor, Georgi! Remember? I work at the hospital here."

"Well, if you're a doctor, why should you want to harm me? You've got your ten million pounds, haven't you? So I presume you don't need anything more from me? Why not just let me go? I can't do you any harm. You've sworn that oath, haven't you?"

She laughed again her delightful laugh. "Oh, you are so persuasive, Georgi, but I'm not sure it would be safe to let you go. I'm not sure it would be safe even to let you live!"

George's stomach churned again, a sensation he was getting inordinately accustomed to and he didn't like it one bit. "Not safe," he protested, "but why? I promise you I *will* keep my mouth shut." He was beginning to feel this was for real now, the options were closing fast.

"Georgi, you misunderstand me, I'm not talking about me being unsafe, I'm talking about you. You're not safe to let out. I owe it to the rest of the world not to set a beast like you loose on the rampage again! You're the biggest beast in the valley, remember?" Oh, she was so good at taking the piss and she did it all in such a sweet way as if butter wouldn't melt in her mouth!

"What the fuck are you talking about?" he shouted. "I'm not a beast, I'm a human being!"

She looked at him askance. "Georgi!" she exclaimed, "what an admission! That isn't like you! You said you were the king of the jungle!" She wagged a reproving finger. "You really should stop contradicting yourself!"

"People will know," he cried, "they'll come looking for me." His voice betrayed his panic.

"Your business associates, Georgi? Do you think so? Don't you think they'll do what businessmen do the world over? Divide up your share, what's left of it, that is, have a drink on you, a wake you call it, don't you? And then move on to the next deal. Isn't this the way sharks behave, Georgi? They are always moving, always feeding? Isn't this how you saw yourself?" It wasn't the right time to think it but he knew what she was saying and it was all too true. "You see, they don't care, people like that. This thing about you being human beings! You forfeited most of your humanity. You only know people who care about money. They have nothing else in their lives."

George was growing frantic now. His strategy wasn't working. Zoya was toying with him, giving the impression of listening but just to torment him further. "My wife," he said, "she'll want to know what happened to me." When he thought about it he realised that at least was true, little as he deserved it. The only decent thing there had ever been in his life and he had to be tied up, a prisoner in a foreign city, talking to a homicidal witch doctor, before the penny had dropped!

"Ah yes," she replied, "your estranged wife. I feel you are right, she may shed a tear for you, although God knows why, but part of the grief will be assuaged by the knowledge that you died in the depths of depravity, because I can assure you that this is the way I will make it look."

"What? What do you mean?"

"Oh hush, Georgi. You know I have to make it look for our police chief that you are just another tourist who liked the fleshpots too much. In my position you'd so exactly the same."

"Jen'll see through that for sure!"

"Really? I rather had the impression it would be just another disappointment of the sort you are accustomed to making her handle. Anyway, I'm sure she will console herself with the insurance money. I like to think I'm doing her a favour." She was staring at him. "Georgi," she said quietly, "the thing about hypnosis is that it doesn't make you act against your own nature. It actually brings out things you try and repress." He returned her gaze suspiciously, wondering what she was driving at now. "Do you remember I was telling you the Lithuanian story of a prince who was warned not to go in a certain room in his wife's castle? I didn't tell you how that story ended, did I? We were interrupted."

He knew this was tied up with his own fate. He was going to learn now what would happen to him. He couldn't take his drowsy eyes off her. "Go on." Even to him his voice was slurred.

"Well, three times the prince fought the soulless man and three times he lost. Each time the soulless one bested him and stabbed him with his sword. The last time, the soulless man became tired of the prince's persistence, so he did not just run him through, he chopped off his head and cut him to pieces, leaving him like a pile of mincemeat by the road for the crows to eat. Then he kidnapped his wife and forced her to be his woman and he usurped the prince's inheritance. He had everything. His conquest was complete. The prince was annihilated."

She stopped talking. "Is that it?" George slurred again after a few moments' silence.

"It is for now," she replied. She ran her tongue over her lips, still teasing him. She stood up slowly, sexily, and walked away from him towards the cupboard, exaggerating each flow of her hips. "So, afterwards you'd walk away, would you? You wouldn't say anything?" The constriction of his arms must have made him pass out for a few moments because Zoya was sitting on the side of the bath again and he hadn't noticed her move. She was speaking but he couldn't hear. His ears were under water. He lifted himself up slightly, feeling the pain in his wrists, listening hard. "What about God? Do you think of God at all?"

He realized it was his last hope, the total opposite of his usual deny, deny, deny philosophy: total confession. "God, he's a joke. What did he ever do for anyone? You can't sit around waiting for God to do your dirty work for you. You've got to get up and do it yourself. Life's a jungle. People are predators. It's kill or be killed. That's what life is, kid. Don't let anyone tell you different. You take care of yourself in this world cos no one ain't going to look after yous. Sure, I've ripped people off, I've papered the walls with money I've taken off fuckwits. The poor are the easiest to get it off. They're always trying to better themselves. Always willing to take a chance. They'll stake their life savings on a gamble that might get them out of the hole they're in. Most of the time they don't see you coming. They want to believe yous. Even now some of them will swear it wasn't a con, it was just bad luck that it didn't work. We never have any luck they say. You nod and agree with them and laugh all the way to the bank. Serves them right really, it's their own greed that gets them into bother. Like yous I see it as a kind of service, just like birds of prey do. Just think of the disease there would be if there weren't vultures cleaning up all the dead flesh!"

"What do you truly think about your life, Georgi?"

He sighed. "Right now I think it's pretty rotten."

She smiled. "You're being witty again."

"No, kid, no. That's it. I don't just mean this. I mean my whole life. It's shit. It really is."

"So what would you do about it if you had another chance?"

"Just change, be different."

"It's good that you've come to that realisation," she said. She held up the surgical scalpel.

"I knew you were a real doctor," he said.

She smiled. "Well, didn't I just warn you!" She leaned over towards him, the scalpel held between the thumb and first two fingers of her left hand. She flicked the silver knife downwards towards his bound, upturned right wrist, then, ever so gently, she drew the blade across. It was a careful, precise cut, in the line of the old wound. He realised then what that might have been, a dry run, a warning! They could have been telling him to get out of there, scurry off home, his tail between his legs! But what if he had? Would none of this have happened? Just a night on the tiles and a salutary lesson? Could they have been giving him a chance? If so, the message had been too subtle. It always is. He looked at the sliver of blood. Because of the constriction it didn't spurt out but it stained the water as it shimmied like a dragon into the depths. Gently, as if it were an act of kindness, the night doctor cut the other wrist in the same, pre-ordained line and watched the act repeated. Then she cut the bonds which held his wrists. His hands slumped into the water. He watched from a distance as first it grew orange and then a wispier brown.

It was like standing in a different world and observing the man dying in the water, like a dummy deflating, the flesh hanging loosely as the force ebbed from him. Having trained as a doctor in the Eastern Bloc, she had seen much worse and so she exhibited no sign of pity.

CHAPTER 17

The rickety old white Trabant, both wings bodged with unpainted, unsmoothed filler, lurched over the kerb on to the miles and miles of white sand somewhere near the town of Palanga in western Lithuania. The driver was Vytautus. He had a particular mission - something in the body disposal department. The boot lid of the vehicle was tied down by string because it wouldn't close properly. He scanned the sands ahead for a likely spot. There weren't many people out on the beach. It was a blowy day and the wind off the shore was whipping up the waves. The few passers-by, walking their dogs or simply strolling along, turned towards the sea to keep the sand out of their eyes. Out on the Klaipeda Highway the lorries thundered past, heading for Panevezys and Vilnius. The ground shook as they trundled by on roads in need of re-laying. He'd had a good journey, getting away early so he'd missed most of the heavy traffic. He hoped now it wasn't just his luck for a policeman to stop him for driving on the sand. He could scarcely say: "I have to dispose of a body." He laughed at the thought. She was a card, the night doctor.

His eyes searched ahead. She'd described a breakwater which came straight off the land out to the sea - as far as the car could drive on the sand. Where the breakwater joined the land there was a ditch which brought surface water down from the field drains which served the vast forests adjacent to the shore. "Ah!" he exclaimed as he saw the wavy black outline of the breakwater straggling down to the water margin. It was hazy in the sunlight and seemed to float like a meniscus line as he stared at it.

The Trabant trundled on, its tyres sinking into the sand. The coughing and spluttering engine caused him to fear it would give up the ghost, but eventually he reached the breakwater. It was higher than it had seemed from a distance but shrank as it approached the waterline. That left sufficient room for him to manouevre round the bottom posts. The sand was even softer there and he feared suddenly, with one of those irrational fears, that it was quicksand. He had to get to the other side because the night doctor had told him there would be no people on that side – no one to watch what he was doing and inform on him to the authorities. "Would it not be best done at night?" he had asked her, but she had laughed at his fears and replied, "No, that wouldn't be proper at all." She knew best, the night doctor. There was nothing she didn't know. Many years he had been a porter in the hospital and he had never known a doctor like the night doctor. She had the power of healing. She could work miracles.

Its windscreen wipers warding off the assault of flying wet sand, the vehicle struggled round the ramparts of the breakwater and moved sluggishly with wheel-spin up the other side. There, as she had said, was a ditch where the water came off the land. Today it was dry but in the rainy season it would be a raging torrent and there was no way the vehicle would have got round that breakwater. He got out of the car and started to walk along it, looking down into it as he did so and from time to time glancing furtively round to ensure he was not being watched. He wasn't sure how dangerous this was, but he was doing it for the night doctor. He would have laid down his life for the night doctor. Vytautus stopped in his tracks. The end was in sight. He'd found the place she'd mentioned, a deep depression in the ditch, filled with water. Dutifully, he returned to the car. He removed from it the black body bag. Breathing heavily he carried it to the ditch. He put it down on the lip then, taking out his Stanley knife, he cut it at the head until a face appeared. He looked at it curiously. It was a European male. There was nothing remotely surprising about that. European males died all the time in the hospital, but he couldn't think of any that were buried out here. He stared harder then realised he recognised the face. Its open, glassy eyes stared vacantly into space with no hint of acknowledgment of its surroundings. "Ah, the ass'ole from the airport," he said. "Couldn't hold his liquor!"

Obeying his instructions he cut the bag down to the shoulders just so the arms would be free, then, using all his strength, he rolled it over the edge. It went over horizontally and then twisted and toppled vertically down. He watched it go with satisfaction until it plummeted into the murky quicksand beneath. It was a good price. Who'd have thought this foreigner with the bleak blue eyes would be worth ten thousand litas? He could as easily have put him on the trolley and put him in the furnace at the hospital but she wanted him stuck out here, because this way, presumably, there were no forms to fill in, no bureaucracy to satisfy. He didn't know; she'd never levelled with him, nor would he expect her to. If you just did your job and everyone else did theirs ninety-nine times out of a hundred the right result would come about as if by clockwork.

The body began to succumb to the sand. The corpse had a sort of surprised look in its eyes as Vytautus waved to it before turning on his heel and walking away. Above his head, a gull screamed accusingly. George heard the bird's cry and jerked awake. "Aaaah!" he screamed as memory came back. He stared around unbelievingly. It was daylight and he was out in the open air. The space seemed to be enclosed, claustrophobic, but so cold, like a Baltic winter. He wondered what they'd done with him this time. He tried to look down at his bound body, remembering the slashed wrists. He was in a kind of bag, like a soldier's body bag! But it was all right. He was alive. He didn't know how or why, he could even remember slipping away in that bath of warm water and not caring about it, not caring at all, being beyond all toil and trouble, escaping from a rotten life. He felt a twinge of disappointment then suddenly found himself sinking. "Help!" he screamed.

Vytautus had just slammed the car door when there came once again the gull's cry. There was something odd about it, worthy of exploration. He opened the door, exasperated but inquisitive, got out and looked up. He did a double take. It wasn't a gull, it was a hovering bird, a hawk. Perhaps it had strayed from the land in search of food. He eyed it intently. Somewhere he could hear a dog bark. Getting back in the vehicle, he turned on the engine. The bird squawked again. He looked up out of the windscreen. He couldn't see it. He drove slowly down the sand, round the breakwater where it was still soft and up the other side. The wheels felt as if they would not grip properly but he chugged on and eventually the vehicle pulled itself clear. He headed down towards the gap in the beach leading to the car park. The sun was beginning to stretch over the eastern sky.

Simultaneously George looked up and saw a kestrel hovering above him. Then he heard a dog barking and he turned to see it on the bank, a little, yellow-coloured dog. It was half crouched, its teeth bared. A crab scuttled back into its hole in the sand. George felt the suction as he moved and realised it was only his earlier inertia which had saved him from being dragged down into the yellow mud. In the bank to his left there was a tree root. If only he could reach it he might be able to pull himself out. The dog barked even more furiously as if it understood the unfolding drama. He tried to stay calm. Stretching slowly, feeling the suction with each movement, he finally worked himself far enough over to make a lunge for the root. The dog yelped and took off as if it had been scalded but, hooking his arm round the gnarled limb, George pulled himself free, easing himself out of the body bag which immediately wrinkled up and, with a sucking sound, disappeared into the yellow ooze. He was surprised to find himself clothed. They must have put his clothes back on. The attention they paid to detail!

Circumnavigating the bog, he walked back down to the beach. He passed the breakwater and began to jog along the sand. There were people out walking, it seemed a popular place and he looked around to see if he could see the dog and its owner. He wanted to thank someone, although he didn't quite know why. Neither was he sure of what he was going to do next. Then his mobile phone rang. It had been re-charged. The screen said Home. This time he took the call.

CHAPTER 18

One of the crap roles George took on as part of his
"punishment" was tripping round the provinces looking
after the bank's far-flung investments. Marty was in a
gruff but relatively good mood when he got back. It
turned out another investment had come up trumps but,
secretly, George thought he was going soft. He would
have killed himself, so to speak. Back in the old days so
would Marty - have killed him, that is. The days passed
in the usual blur of misinformation while they decided
what to do with him. He had the feeling that his
colleagues were looking at him pityingly, hoping he
wasn't evidence of how it all ended up. But he didn't
care. He was back with Jen and the kids. He'd stayed in
the job because he had to do something but he intended
to retire from it as quickly as he could and that was
partly because his colleagues were taking the piss.

The punishment, when it came, was one move up from
being the office tea boy. A lot of these investments
were legit, a kind of hedge against the riskier business,
and they were invariably boring. He got them all to deal
with now. He wasn't trusted with anything cutting edge.

But in spite of his complaints, George secretly
welcomed the trips away from his colleagues. Then,
one summer's day he was up in Edinburgh, chairing a

joint meeting of the Scottish bond holders – the Haggis Run as the bank knew it. He'd done it many times in the old days so it went like clockwork. It was festival time in the Scottish capital and the festivities and art shows spilled out into the provinces. Once he would have been the life and soul of the party, taking the piss out of the arty-farty types but nonetheless joining in the fun, particularly if there was fanny about. Now he just couldn't be arsed. He was strictly the straight man, saving his impudent sense of humour for home, where he had a captive audience even if they all liked to take the mickey out of him. But there was something missing. He knew that. He had left it behind him in Lithuania. Maybe it was like his manhood, that precious macho self-confidence without which he had once been unable to function. If things weren't quite that bleak now, he still hankered after that old self from time to time. He wondered what had happened to the boy.

One morning in his hotel, someone pushed a leaflet under the door. He picked it up, gave it a cursory glance, one which made him register sufficient surprise to wheel round to the door and see if the delivery person was still visible. Unfortunately he was gazing at a typical hotel corridor, one which might have been an extension of the Empty Quarter, so he closed it again and studied the drop. It was of the mass-produced type and advertised the fact that, on the front a few miles away, the Pier Pavilion, as part of the Festival, was putting on a Baltic Arts night. According to the leaflet, there were to be folk songs and dances and some theatricals from Belarus and each of the Baltic States, Latvia. Estonia and Lithuania. Coincidence or what? George couldn't remember mentioning his interest in such things when he'd booked into the hotel but it was possible his very efficient secretary (who secretly did half of his job for him, the half which amounted to real work, he was fond of saying) had included it in the forward information. She was always trying to cheer him up and maybe she thought, too, that he'd left something behind in Lithuania but thought it something more obvious like a love interest. In a way she was right but he had to admit it was a peculiar way. He couldn't forget the night doctor but he knew darn well it would be best if he did.

It was that night, when he was sitting alone again in his hotel room, listening to the noise from the street carnival outside and feeling like an extra-terrestrial after the obligatory phone home, that he remembered the leaflet. It had assumed the character of a personal invitation from providence to do something about the dead-and-alive state into which he had fallen. The idea that he could was clutching at straws, he knew, but anything was worth a try! He crept out of the hotel, avoided the street party, and caught a bus. After a ride down to the waterfront he found himself walking along the promenade and there was no doubt he at least meant to check out the Baltic Arts show. He expected it would prove another disappointment. On a sudden impulse and in spite of his snazzy Italian shoes (he still dressed well; old habits die hard was another thing he would say to anyone who listened) he stepped down on to the sands.

An impression he'd never experienced previously suddenly assailed him. Funny, he could have been back on that beach in Palanga, walking the miles towards the Norway ferry at Klaipeda. The folk out walking with their kids and their dogs looked the same; the wind blew the same; the sand whipping up and stinging his face, getting in his eyes, up his nostrils, felt the same. Even the breakwater he had to clamber over looked the same. Out at sea regiments of white horses charged ashore. Just as back then they looked like hordes of the Teutonic Knights with their white surcoats and the black cross where the wave broke. He remembered how Zoya had talked during that dinner party long ago?

"At the battle of Lake Peipus, which is now on the border between Latvia and Russia, the Knights with their gigantic horses, their flowing cloaks, faceless helmets and black-crossed shields, crossed the frozen lake in the dark."

The thought occurred to him jarringly hard that he hadn't really crossed those sands, he'd just imagined the journey. What proof was there now he'd travelled that way? What proof is there anyone's travelled anywhere? It's all in the past, it's all in that other country. But what if he was remembering in a delirious state another walk and confusing it with the delusion that he had made *that* walk *then*? Or confusing the imagined memory of that walk then with another now? This could go on ad infinitum and he'd still be no nearer the truth. Sooner or later you had to go with your five senses. The sequence made him feel so depressed that he thought of just waiting until nightfall, throwing himself off the pier and then swimming for as long as he could towards the east. Sooner or later he would develop hypothermia, twenty, thirty minutes perhaps, and that would be the end. He would carry something heavy so that when he sank he would go straight down and his body would never be recovered. Maybe a mermaid from Atlantis would come for him and they'd live happily ever after. Ha! Chance'd be a fine thing.

As these doomsday thoughts subsided he began to think that, probably the reason he was confusing this stretch of sand with one in another time and another place was he couldn't remember anything that happened yesterday or even earlier today. He could remember hazily that he'd been to a meeting but he couldn't for the life of him remember who had been there or what they had discussed. Funny, he knew all those guys but they might as well have been dead for all he could recall of them. They had indistinct, blubbery faces, which would come into focus and then slip out again. Had that happened when they were present, when he was in their so-called company and he in theirs? That's where it fell apart. He couldn't remember but he thought that generally he went through the motions all right; he didn't do anything drastically wrong; he just wasn't his old self. He wondered if he was experiencing the beginning of a nervous breakdown but was that a contradiction in terms? The something struck him with the force of an epiphany: "she's kept part of me!" he shouted aloud to himself. He looked round, shocked by his own outburst. It was as well he was alone on this stretch of sand, but now he could indulge his fantasy and, the more he did so, the less fantastic it seemed. It was that story she had told: the one about the soul stolen away.

At the end of the beach there was a series of steps up to the pier. They were never-ending. They went up to a path, it wound round, met some more steps and then you climbed again, repeating the procedure time and time again. In his anger he took the lower stages quickly and then stopped, his heart beating. Phew! Half way up he stopped and mopped his brow. He hadn't remembered going that far down the other side. It had been a gentle slope, long but gentle. Plodding up here was like going to the top of Everest. He'd be needing oxygen soon! A large building, the kind of pleasure pavilion you find in the average British seaside town, appeared as if out of a haze and he saw he was on the sea wall. The waves crashed up hungrily beneath him. A bird squawked and he glanced up to see a gull, riding the wind like a lanthorn. From the beach a dog barked. A queue had formed outside the pavilion. Some were youngsters but most of them looked like pensioners. They seemed harmless enough. He didn't usually need to pluck up courage to ask but it was an effort this time. "What's going on?" he said to the queue generally. No one answered so he tried to revert to his cheeky former self: "does anyone speak English?" Everyone looked at him strangely. He was aware suddenly of a pretty girl handing out leaflets. She was wearing an ornate dress of different colours and he was captivated by it. Ignoring the crowd, he grinned at the girl and pointed to the fliers. "Can I have one?" he asked.

She smiled, her big white teeth right in his face. "Of course," she replied. She thumbed off a leaflet. It was just like the leaflet except it was a postcard. "You can post it back to your loved ones." Her smile remained ravishing, her English impeccable.

"What's the costume, love?" he asked her.

"It is my country's national dress," she replied.

"What country is that then?" He knew it already, of course. "Lithuania?" he added before she could reply.

"Yes, how clever of you to know! Have you been there?"

He nodded. "I have," he replied.

She clapped her hands in genuine joy. "Oh, it is a beautiful country!" Her face shone with enthusiasm.

He was reminded of Zoya. "Beautiful," he admitted, "but dangerous too." She looked as if his comment had taken her by surprise. He changed the subject: "can you tell me what this is for?" He indicated the queue.

"This queue?" the girl replied. "This is to see the Waste Disposal Team! They are very famous in our country!" She pointed at a notice board outside the pavilion, which George could see now was a small theatre but he was having trouble not hyperventilating.

"The Waste Disposal Team?" he repeated, "what's that when it's at home?" He tried to make a joke of it but wondered if she'd notice he was trembling.

The girl smiled indulgently. "It's a theatrical group," she said, "I guess over here you'd call it alternative theatre!"

"A theatrical group!" He was bowled over. "Professional actors you mean?"

She nodded. His mind was beginning to analyse this information, bring it into the data bank of his other experiences and sometimes new data does not fit with what is already there; sometimes it simply doesn't add up to anything tangible, but this information wasn't like that. This made him think. He couldn't quite grasp it; he couldn't see why it should be symmetrical, not yet anyway, but it didn't jar. It didn't shout out at him, *that can't be right.* "Well," the girl responded, "no one can make a living out of the theatre in Lithuania! It isn't Hollywood, you know!" She laughed as if the thought

260

was absurd. "No, worse luck! All these actors are part-timers. They've all got other jobs as well."

"Tell me about it," George said, "what, you mean some of them are doctors and nurses, eh?"

"Well, yes," the girl replied, puzzled by his knowledge, "that's quite right. How did you know?"

He shrugged. "Ah, lucky guess. What's your name anyway, kid?"

"Natalie," she replied.

"Okay, Natalie, what's your story?" he asked, "how come you're with the Waste Disposal Team?"

The girl's eyes shone. "It's always been my ambition," she explained, "my grandfather is kind of the roadie." He nodded, thinking how strange it would be if it was that daft old bugger who'd picked him up at the airport. Then Natalie asked, "Are you coming in?" Her blue eyes, framed beneath the blond fringe of her bobbed hair, opened wide in innocent invitation. He shrugged and followed her. He wasn't sure if he was doing the right thing but what else was there? The truth was, though, he was intrigued and also more than a little scared. "Are you interested in the theatre?" she asked as he handed over his cash at the box office.

"I'm getting there, in my old age," George replied

ruefully. "Why don't you come in and interpret for me?" he added.

"Okay," she replied with her delightful smile. George was going to pay for her but she took his arm gently just above the wrist and added, "I'm staff, I don't pay." George smiled and nodded. "Have you ever tried acting?" she bantered as they walked towards the door into the auditorium.

"No," George laughed, "I'd be useless. Funny though. A Lithuanian lady once said I should go on the stage. Too late but, for me to start thinking of things like that."

"You're joking!" she replied. "We have one member of our cast who is in his sixties, he used to be a soldier, you're never too old!" George couldn't hide his surprise. Who was she talking about? Surely not the general? "No, seriously," she went on, "we're always looking for new recruits."

"Don't you have to be Lithuanian?" George asked sarcastically. He licked his lips nervously, his mouth suddenly dry.

"Oh no, we're far more catholic in our approach than that!" Natalie gave a shrug of her narrow shoulders.

The auditorium was already two thirds full. Newcomers were arriving all the time. George and Natalie took their seats in a stall. George would have preferred to be on the end of a row in case he had a sudden urge to bolt but his companion led him towards the centre, to get a better view of the stage. Once the audience was seated the lights in the auditorium went down and the play started. It was a costume drama. George recognised Aldona straight away. He didn't really need Natalie to explain her role as a princess. Then the principal boy arrived. He played the prince. "This is an old Lithuanian folk tale," Natalie said.

"I know," George replied.

She looked impressed. "You know everything!"

The prince proved as curious as George had been. He couldn't resist looking in the room. There was a dead man lying there. George sniggered. "It's the general!" he chortled and Natalie looked at him in wonder.

"How do you know that?"

"All it needs now is the Scouser! At least she didn't get that allusion.

The prince appeared to revive the dead man. The girl translated for George. It was magic apparently. "The dead man's the king," she murmured.

"Yeah, I know, kid, he's a soulless king!"

"You have to tell me how you know all this!"

"Instinct!" She looked at him with a new respect and he gave her his now traditional wan smile.

The play drew his attention. He had the queerest feeling it was meant especially for him. He wasn't afraid of his adversaries on stage. They couldn't know of his presence. He felt like thumbing his nose and going na-na-na-na-na but shuddered when he remembered they must think he was buried alive at the bottom of the quicksand. It gave him even more of a thrill to be here, to have put one over on them. Only the general was a bit of a ham, but the audience seemed to love it as he clowned his head off. It was only in the fight scenes with the prince that he came into his own. He was obviously an expert swordsman.

The story went the way Zoya had narrated to him when he'd had his preview, but then it took a turn. The wife, who had been abducted by the wicked, soulless king, collected up the mortal remains of her husband after the king, tired with the younger man's persistence, had cut him up like a side of beef. Loud, mournful music followed, then a flurry of mist from the special effects. The lights went down, it was pitch black, fifteen seconds or so went by and then another actor came on dressed as a large feathery bird. As soon as he turned and faced the audience, George recognised the same actor who had played the principal boy, doubling up in the tradition of the old theatre companies. He'd done a quick change from being mincemeat to taking flight on feathery wings, drawn airborne across the stage on invisible wires. Alighting, the bird danced with an artistry, which, even George, who was no culture vulture, recognised as brilliant. Then it poured water from its beak on the remains of the prince, played now by some actor who just had to lie there pretending to be dead. George laughed when he saw it was the general again. He got all the dead parts. The audience thought it hilarious and roared its delight. Then there was a thunderclap and the stage went dark. Figures whirled around for fifteen seconds or so and then, when the special effects were over, the eye was drawn back to the prone form on the floor. The corpse began to stir. Natalie whispered that the moisture from the bird's beak had been full of magic potions. They had brought the prince back to life.

When the prone body sat up the huge bird had metamorphosed back into the principal boy. Then an actor dressed as a yellow dog ran on to the stage, giving a good impression of barking. It was the colour of the dog on the sand bank, and the mutt at the apartment. The more he stared at it the more he appreciated that the actor playing the big, lolloping animal was familiar to him, then he realised it was the Scouser and this time he roared with such laughter that everyone along the row looked at him in surprise but, of course, they didn't get the joke.

Natalie was unperturbed by his reaction but it was she

who brought him back to earth. "It is essential," the girl said with due seriousness, "that the prince should not kick the dog or attack the hawk, because they are the only ones who will help him."

George looked at her uncomfortably. The prince, meanwhile, revitalised by the magical potion, had made himself known to his loving wife. He whispered into her ear, putting her up to some skullduggery, which would enable his resurrected self to claim the king's lost soul and take back his place on earth.

The play was then replete with sexual innuendo, which held the audience spellbound and silent as if they dare not acknowledge their feelings, just as George felt uncomfortable with his own. The princess used all her arts and wiles, of which he was more than appreciative because he had enjoyed them for himself and knew she possessed them in abundance. Finally she discovered from the unsuspecting king, who, despite his soulless state, was kindly disposed towards his young mistress and her obvious physical charms, precisely what had become of his immortal soul. It lay at the bottom of a sandy lake, he told her, and it resounded clearly to George, because he had nearly done precisely that. The complication was that the soul was contained within an egg which lay on the lake bed.

Diving to the bottom of the lake, a scene which was carried off against a backdrop of blue water, sectioned so as to show the sandy bottom, and the sound of crashing waves, the prince was able to find the place and so regain the soul with the help of the dog and the hawk. As soon as he had taken it from the egg, which had protected it, the old king fell ill. In no time this man of great martial prowess became a weakling. The prince intruded into his bedchamber and, without any compunction, tortured him and then murdered him in his sick bed. It was amazing how brutal these fables were!

"That was cowardly," George said angrily, "taking advantage of the poor guy when he's down!"

"Poor guy?" Natalie replied and there was no doubting the irony.

The two lovers, much to the delight of the audience, were then reunited. Despite the girl's words George still felt angry for the fate of the king. Why did he have to die like that all alone? Everyone deserves some comfort in his hour of need!

The curtain came down to immense applause. George sat as still as a standing stone, locked into the memory of the performance, trying to figure it out or, more particularly, what it meant for him, because it could have been put on just for him. Everyone else there was irrelevant.

Then the curtain went up again. Holding hands in a line, the actors presented themselves and bowed. The principal boy came forward, still wearing a head-dress, of gorgeous feathers, evidence of duality. She had the face of an angel: beautiful, unearthly, and terrible. In her hand she held something oval. She stretched it out towards the audience. It seemed monstrously large - as big as an ostrich's egg. The audience clapped and cheered. She smiled then made as if to drop it. She did this three times and each time the spectators cheered louder. There were loud cries of encore! George sat in suspended animation.

When she let the egg go, the actors all leaned forward simultaneously, as if presenting the piece de resistance to the audience, all of whom rose, except for George. He sat still. It took an age for the object to hit the boards.

So long that he didn't notice everyone get up and leave until there was only him left in the darkened stalls. When the egg did land it smashed into a thousand glittering fragments. His eyes were glued to where the yolk should be. He expected to see something emerge and he wasn't quite sure if it would be solid like a diamond or insubstantial as vapour, taking flight like a bird. But he was disappointed. There was nothing there. Absolutely nothing at all.

CPSIA information can be obtained
at www.ICGtesting.com
Printed in the USA
LVHW111511150919
631121LV00003B/669/P

9 781500 984847